# THE AMETHYST CITY

# Borgo Press Books by JOHN RUSSELL FEARN

*1,000-Year Voyage: A Science Fiction Novel* * *Anjani the Mighty: A Lost Race Novel* (Anjani #2) * *Black Maria, M.A.: A Classic Crime Novel* (Black Maria #1) * *The Crimson Rambler: A Crime Novel* * *Don't Touch Me: A Crime Novel* * *Dynasty of the Small: Classic Science Fiction Stories* * *The Empty Coffins: A Mystery of Horror* * *The Fourth Door: A Mystery Novel* * *From Afar: A Science Fiction Mystery* * *Fugitive of Time: A Classic Science Fiction Novel* * *The G-Bomb: A Science Fiction Novel* * *The Genial Dinosaur* (Herbert the Dinosaur #2) * *The Gold of Akada: A Jungle Adventure Novel* (Anjani #1) * *Here and Now: A Science Fiction Novel* * *Into the Unknown: A Science Fiction Tale* * *Last Conflict: Classic Science Fiction Stories* * *Legacy from Sirius: A Classic Science Fiction Novel* * *The Man from Hell: Classic Science Fiction Stories* * *The Man Who Was Not: A Crime Novel* * *Manton's World: A Classic Science Fiction Novel* * *Moon Magic: A Novel of Romance* (as Elizabeth Rutland) * *The Murdered Schoolgirl: A Classic Crime Novel* (Black Maria #2) * *One Remained Seated: A Classic Crime Novel* (Black Maria #3) * *One Way Out: A Crime Novel* (with Philip Harbottle) * *Pattern of Murder: A Classic Crime Novel* * *Reflected Glory: A Dr. Castle Classic Crime Novel* * *Robbery Without Violence: Two Science Fiction Crime Stories* * *Rule of the Brains: Classic Science Fiction Stories* * *Shattering Glass: A Crime Novel* * *The Silvered Cage: A Scientific Murder Mystery* * *Slaves of Ijax: A Science Fiction Novel* * *Something from Mercury: Classic Science Fiction Stories* * *The Space Warp: A Science Fiction Novel* * *A Thing of the Past* (Herbert the Dinosaur #1) * *Thy Arm Alone: A Classic Crime Novel* (Black Maria #4) * *The Time Trap: A Science Fiction Novel* * *Vision Sinister: A Scientific Detective Thriller* * *Voice of the Conqueror: A Classic Science Fiction Novel* * *What Happened to Hammond? A Scientific Mystery* * *Within That Room!: A Classic Crime Novel*

## *THE GOLDEN AMAZON SAGA*

1. *World Beneath Ice* * 2. *Lord of Atlantis* * 3. *Triangle of Power* * 4. *The Amethyst City* * 5. *Daughter of the Amazon* * 6. *Quorne Returns* * 7. *The Central Intelligence* * 8. *The Cosmic Crusaders* * 9. *Parasite Planet* * 10. *World Out of Step* * 11. *The Shadow People* * 12. *Kingpin Planet* * 13. *World in Reverse* * 14. *Dwellers in Darkness* * 15. *World in Duplicate* * 16. *Lords of Creation* * 17. *Duel with Colossus* * 18. *Standstill Planet* * 19. *Ghost World* * 20. *Earth Divided* * 21. *Chameleon Planet* (with Philip Harbottle)

# THE AMETHYST CITY

## THE GOLDEN AMAZON SAGA, BOOK FOUR

## JOHN RUSSELL FEARN

Edited by Philip Harbottle

THE BORGO PRESS

MMXIII

# THE AMETHYST CITY

FIRST BORGO PRESS EDITION

Published by Wildside Press LLC

www.wildsidebooks.com

# DEDICATION

For Gordon Rix, a true fan of the Amazon

# CONTENTS

# THE GOLDEN AMAZON
## by Philip Harbottle

In 1943 British writer John Russell Fearn decided to quit writing for the American pulp science fiction magazines, and to concentrate instead on books for the English market. Within a very few years he became established as a leading novelist in several genres, not only science fiction, but also mystery and detective fiction, and westerns.

His first new SF novel, *The Golden Amazon*, was published by World's Work in April 1944. In this story, a little girl of three years of age is made the subject of an idealistic scientist's illegal glandular experiments. The scientist's dream is to end world wars by creating a woman devoid of the usual lusts and frailties of mankind, who upon reaching maturity would institute a benign scientific rule. But the apparently successful experiment has a flaw: it instills into the girl a hatred for all men, and a ruthless cruelty. Her supernatural scientific gifts enable her to master atomic power, and practically leads her to destroy the world. She breaks the will and strength of men, and elevates women to positions of wealth and power. She also discovers human synthesis, and by this means she is able to escape retribution when she is eventually overthrown. She is seen to collapse and die, a victim of consuming ketabolism, echoing the memorable finale of Rider Haggard's *She*. In actuality, it was only her synthetic image, and this paved the way for the *Golden Amazon Returns*, and further sequels

Fearn sold reprint rights in the first novel to the prestigious Canadian magazine, the Toronto *Star Weekly*. The magazine carried a special Comics Supplement, the centre section of which was a 'complete novel', published in newspaper format. Aimed at a general readership, the novels were written by the top popular novelists of the day, including John Dickson Carr, Ellery Queen, and P. G. Wodehouse. They sold hundreds of thousands of copies, and the novels were syndicated to several American newspapers in the Maine and New York areas. The Amazon novels enjoyed extraordinary popularity (especially with Canadian housewives), and ran for the next sixteen years following the appearance of the first novel in the March 3, 1945 issue, ending with Fearn's sudden death in September 1960, aged only fifty-two. His final two Amazon novels appeared posthumously.

During Fearn's lifetime, only the first six novels were published in British hardcover editions from the World's Work in England, after appearing in the *Star Weekly*. This was because the publishers discontinued their entire fiction line in 1954. However, the Amazon novels continued to appear in the *Star Weekly*, eventually notching up twenty-four titles.

Fearn had resold paperback rights to the Canadian publisher Harlequin Books, but after publishing only the first three titles, they stopped publishing SF and other genre fiction to concentrate on their famous Romances line.

Meanwhile, as early as 1949, Fearn had realized that the Amazon series had the potential to run indefinitely. This presented him with a problem, however. The 'origin story' of the Golden Amazon was conceived and actually set during the Second World War. Subsequent novels were written during the war and the immediate postwar period, and projected their stories only a few decades into the future.

He very astutely realized that to keep ahead of reality, he needed to move the Amazon *further* into the future—first into the outer solar system, and thence to the stars. So with the seventh novel, he introduced a new main character, Abna of Atlantis—someone as equally intelligent, and even stronger than herself. These dynamics provided him with an *interstellar* canvas, thus ensuring that the series would remain ahead of reality.

Fearn's strategy was a great success, and the Amazon novels retained their popularity, ending only with his tragically early death in 1960. By then he had written a further twenty Amazon novels, and made preliminary notes for his next (which would later be written by Fearn's biographer, Philip Harbottle).

Long after Fearn's death, his entire Amazon series would eventually see print from the pioneering US small press Gryphon Books in limited paperback editions, and later by the Canadian Battered Silicon Dispatch Box small press in their hardcover Omnibus series.

This new Borgo Press paperback series will be the first trade edition of all twenty-one of these later novels by Fearn, beginning with the seventh novel in the original series. First published in 1949 as *Conquest of the Amazon*, I have edited it slightly as *World Beneath Ice* (The Golden Amazon Saga, Book One) so that it can be read and enjoyed by new readers who may be totally unfamiliar with what had gone before. Subsequent novels have also been slightly edited for modern readers.

The publishers hope that this new series may create many more "fans of the Amazon." Meanwhile, any reader interested in seeking out the earlier six Golden Amazon novels will find that they are readily available on the internet, and in numerous earlier paperback and hardcover editions.

\* \* \* \* \* \* \* \* \*

To date, readers can enjoy the following new Borgo Press editions:

### Book One: *World Beneath Ice*

In destroying the threat of an alien invasion, the Golden Amazon had inadvertently caused a decline in the sun's heat, encasing Earth in an ice sheet that threatens to eliminate humanity. The Amazon encounters Abna, a descendant of Atlantis, stronger and even more scientifically advanced than she, and the ruler of an Atlantean colony still surviving in a protected environment on Jupiter. She refuses his offer of marriage, but agrees to form an alliance in order to restore the sun and save the Earth. One thing that Abna has not told the Amazon is that all the females of his race have been wiped out by a bacilli infection....

## Book Two: *Lord of Atlantis*

A gigantic ridge of land rises from the Atlantic floor, causing massive tidal waves on either side of the ocean. Even stranger, both England and America are then assailed by an invasion of prehistoric monsters! A gigantic domed city rests on the newly risen plateau, whilst out in space an alien spacecraft orbits the Earth. Such are the mysteries and challenges facing the Golden Amazon, self-appointed governess of Earth, as she struggles to unravel the maze of mystery that was the deadly legacy of Atlantis!

## Book Three: *Triangle of Power*

The marriage of Violet Ray Brant—better known as The Golden Amazon—and Abna of Atlantis should have ushered in an era of peace and scientific prosperity to the people of Earth. But an unexpected turn of events finds Abna betrayed and marooned on a satellite of Jupiter, and the Amazon flung far beyond the

Solar System. With Earth's two protectors removed, the planet is now at the mercy of another Atlantean, the master scientist Sefnor Quorne....

# CHAPTER ONE
## ATTEMPT TO KILL

The people of Earth and the neighbouring colony worlds were enjoying one of the quietest periods they had ever known. The period when the people had been under the subjection of Sefner Quorne, master-scientist of Jupiter, was mere history. Sefner Quorne had disappeared and with him had gone the menace of his personality.

In fact the latter days of the twenty-first century were quite a pleasant time in which to live. Most of the people knew they owed their lives and present tranquillity to Violet Ray Brant, the Golden Amazon, but so completely did the superwoman disdain praise that there did not seem to be any point in publicly thanking her. In fact, this would have been impractical anyway.

She was 20,000 miles from Earth in her space machine, the *Ultra*. She was just at the close of destroying a small but dangerous planetoid, which had fallen into an orbit about the Earth. Brought to this position by four-dimensional mechanics, the planetoid had been used by the Amazon as a thought reflector, which ingenious scheme had brought Sefner Quorne to disaster and freed Earth from his domination. But that the planetoid should remain as an added satellite of Earth was unthinkable. It was too sensitive an object, and too useful a weapon for enemies.

Now it floated in space in the form of dust, a shimmering grey cloud catching the light of the sun, a cloud that was nothing more than cosmic drift and no longer of use in any form.

"A very necessary job completed, Relka," the Amazon commented, gazing out into space.

Her sole companion was a squat, ugly, crocodile-like man of Jupiter, a clever scientist despite his extraordinary physical vestment. He breathed the Earth-normal atmosphere aboard the Amazon's ship as easily as his native ammoniated hydrogen, thanks to an amazingly adaptive metabolism. He did not respond to the Amazon's comment. Instead, he was looking at the Amazon intently, struck by her queer expression. In all the time he had known her, he had never seen her looking introspective. Yet that mood seemed to be gripping her now.

The prominence-girdled sun threw her features into strong relief, features so breathtakingly lovely they were phenomenal. But the Golden Amazon was no ordinary woman. Science had made of her a creature of tremendous scientific attainments, and matched it with an incomparably perfect body and almost eternal youth. The Golden Amazon was more of a legend than a woman. Only one thing stopped her being altogether desirable—the streak of ruthless cruelty in her makeup. It was this that isolated her from normal beings—isolated her from everybody indeed save one. And he was dead.

"I find it difficult to understand your mood, Amazon," Relka commented at length, standing by the switchboard. "I had expected you would be particularly cheerful at having destroyed that planetoid; instead, I find you moody, somehow different."

The Amazon started out of her preoccupation and glanced up. It was hard to read anything from the deep violet of her eyes. Though Relka spoke entirely by telepathy, and could read thoughts clearly, he found it impossible to penetrate the mask the Amazon had drawn over her mind. Long since she had discovered how to keep her innermost thoughts private.

"I am entitled sometimes to think of things beyond the immediate present," she answered, giving a little sigh. "I spend most of my life straightening out difficulties for other people—so much so that when I think of something concerning myself, I am looked at in wonder."

"Concerning yourself?" the Jovian repeated. "What could there be?"

The Amazon turned a little in the controlling seat and looked out across space. There on the rim of the solar system floated the magnificent ringed world of Saturn. Relka looked toward it.

"You are thinking of what we saw there? That amethyst city amidst the screaming winds? That something which we could not explain?"

"I am thinking not only of that, Relka, but of Sefner Quorne as well. He is not dead, remember—or at least we have not proved that he is. As long as he remains alive, anything can happen. It's over a year since he disappeared, and nothing has happened in the interval. But I am not comfortable. I never shall be until I know he is obliterated. I have had many enemies, but none so dangerous as Quorne."

The Amazon's extraordinary eyes moved to look at nearer Jupiter. She contemplated it for a long time, going again over the moments that had been her last with Abna, the god-like master of Jupiter. He had died in the collapse of his laboratory, a collapse brought about by Quorne, formerly Abna's chief adviser. Abna! There had only been one man in all the universe whom the Amazon had found it impossible to overcome. Though she pretended indifference to his death, she inwardly knew better. His demise had left a far bigger gap in her life than she had ever thought possible.

"We had better return to Earth," she said, arousing herself. "Our work here is done."

Closing the power switches, she turned the enormous *Ultra* around in a sweeping arc and headed its nose toward the not far distant Earth. Relka was silent for a while, contemplating space, then he turned to the Amazon again.

"Do you think any good purpose could be served by going to Saturn again and exploring it? Quorne may be somewhere on that planet—even in that amethyst city we saw."

"That city was an illusion," the Amazon replied. "It defied all natural laws. Such a beautiful place surrounded by soft green pastures and illuminated by a hidden golden sun just couldn't really be there. Saturn is too far from the sun to have so much light, for one thing, and for another his composition is such that one can only expect raging storms, eternal mist, and complete lack of inhabitants. No, I shall not return to Saturn. From here on I shall pursue my own particular scientific hobbies on Earth. I have lost my taste for roaming."

"Because you have no congenial companion?" Relka asked, and the Amazon flashed him a sharp glance.

"Why do you say that? I couldn't have a more loyal friend than you."

"We work well together, Amazon, because we are of different worlds and cannot, therefore, be physically attracted toward one another. But that is not what you want. I get glimpses of your thoughts sometimes— usually they are centred on Abna. You miss him. You have never forgiven yourself for reviling him when he lived. You would like the chance to do it again."

"I shall never forget Abna," the Amazon admitted ambiguously, then she ceased speaking and her mind was masked again.

She returned the machine to Earth, settling it in the big hangar at the rear of her own residence. The Jovian paused as he opened the hangar's door preparatory to stepping into her home.

"You wish me to remain, Amazon?" he questioned.

"If you will not find it dull, yes. I enjoy your scientific outlook. You can always return to your own planet if you tire of inactivity."

The Jovian nodded, and entered the silence of the great residence, and thereafter it housed two of the most diverse beings it was possible to imagine—one a lovely woman, and the other a terrifying-looking creature with a skin like a crocodile. Yet they understood each other.

In spite of everything, however, the Amazon could not pin herself down to scientific experiments. She made several valiant efforts to interest herself in laboratory technique, exploring matters far beyond the average ken of Earth science, but her heart was not in it. For increasingly long periods she would stand at the bench, her violet eyes fixed on distance, her whole body rigid. Relka was becoming alarmed, though he did his best not to show it.

It was on the morning when the Amazon collapsed suddenly that he felt he had to speak. One moment she was working with an electrical machine; the next, she sprawled helplessly on the floor, and remained there with her eyes wide open and every muscle rigid. With his gigantic strength the Jovian had no difficulty in lifting her. He carried her to a divan in the lounge. But it was four hours before she began to relax and return to normal.

"Amazon, just what is the matter?" his thoughts demanded. "A woman of your flawless physique should not be subject to this kind of thing. You have got to find out the cause!"

She was silent for a while, relaxed on the divan, her eyes half narrowed as she concentrated.

"Physically I was unconscious," she said at length, "but mentally I was completely alive. I saw that amethyst city again. I also saw—Abna." Her voice caught a little. "It was the most extraordinarily vivid dream I have ever known. Yet—just a dream."

"Obviously, Amazon, you have got to rid yourself of these delusions—for that's what they are. They are overriding you, clouding your judgment."

She was silent, reflecting.

"I am your closest friend," Relka continued earnestly. "I have watched you slowly sink into these queer mental wanderings for over a year now. It alarms me. If the Amazon loses her powers of scientific genius, her gift for lightning thinking, what is to happen to everybody? You know perfectly well the System cannot live comfortably without your influence and guiding hand."

The Amazon hesitated over saying something, then glanced up as the bell attached to the front door's photo-electric circuit operated. On a screen over the bell appeared the face of Chris Wilson, head of the Dodd Space Line, and husband of the Amazon's foster sister.

"Come in, Chris," the Amazon said, getting to her feet—and the impact of her voice waves released the front door's complicated lock. Chris Wilson entered the lounge, then hesitated in some alarm, as he saw the mighty Jovian.

"Nothing to be afraid of, Chris," the Amazon said, with a tired smile. "This is Relka of Jupiter—a trusted friend. Relka—Chris Wilson."

"Greetings, Earthman," responded Relka's thoughts, and picking up courage, Chris Wilson came forward. He was a plump, grey-headed man of middle age, neatly dressed, carrying a bulging briefcase.

"I've tried three times to contact you, Vi," he said, "and assumed you were away in space somewhere. I need your signature to one or two documents."

"Concerning what?" The Amazon looked impatient.

"Well, you are still a director of the Dodd Space Line, or had you forgotten?"

"Sorry," the Amazon apologized. "I'm not quite myself."

"I'll go back to the lab," Relka said. "You will wish to talk in private."

He departed and Chris gave the Amazon a puzzled glance as he put his briefcase on the table. She was pacing slowly up and down, pushing an amber-tinted hand through her thick mass of golden hair.

"What's the matter, Vi? It would sound ridiculous if I asked if you are well. You're never anything else."

She glanced at him abstractedly, then without speaking, signed the documents he spread out for her. This done, she raised her unfathomable eyes to look at him.

"Chris, I think Sefner Quorne is at work," she said, and his face clouded.

"There has always been that possibility, of course.

You saw him disappear on Saturn, but never found out any more."

"Things are happening to me," the Amazon continued. "Things that could not happen in the ordinary way because my will and body are normally so strong. I think Quorne is at work with long-distance hypnosis. For a year I have not been complete mistress of myself. I am lazy, have little interest in science, and keep going off in long spells of meditation. Everything culminated this morning when I collapsed. For four hours I was mentally in chains."

Chris Wilson's eyes searched the Amazon's perfect features.

"And what happened during that period? Can you remember?"

"I saw the amethyst city of Saturn, and Abna. I was with him in that city. I spent what I might call the most physically satisfying time of my life there."

"But I thought you said Quorne was back of everything."

"I believe he is. By long-range hypnosis he could suggest anything. He would naturally not give any hint of himself being present, so he used as bait the one person whom I would go to the ends of the universe to see again—Abna. Since Abna is dead, it can only be Quorne who produced that illusion. The reason is plain. He is on Saturn and is trying to lure me there. My reasoning is that for over a year he has been trying to pin me down mentally, and now he has succeeded. He is throwing out a bait, knowing he can never come to Earth and deal with me because I'd be too quick for him."

Chris reflected for a while. "Well, you know more about these things than I do. I suppose it is possible—but I thought Saturn was a planet of hurricanes, gaseous mud, and death. And I also thought the amethyst city, from what you told me earlier, was an illusion."

"Possibly so, but Quorne knows I saw it on my first trip to Saturn when I was chasing him, and he knows how anything unusual excites my curiosity. He might even have transported hypnotic projectors from Jupiter and be using them on Saturn. Whatever the answer, I am satisfied it is a bait."

"I suppose you're right. It—it couldn't be Abna himself, could it?"

The Amazon shook her head. "I have accepted the unalterable fact that he is dead, Chris. No, it's Quorne—and I feel I should accept this challenge, even though I am convinced it is a trick."

"That sounds like taking needless risks, Vi, and I never knew you to do that."

"I have to take it because Quorne has got to be destroyed. No world is safe as long as he lives. I don't know where he is—so I fancy that if I go to Saturn he'll make sure I find him because he'll try to destroy me. It's worth that risk to try to destroy *him*."

Chris smiled a little and patted the Amazon's steel-strong arm.

"I learned long ago not to waste time arguing with you, Vi, so it's up to you," he said. "All I can do is wish you good luck."

With that he turned away and left the lounge. The front door opened automatically for him and closed again. The Amazon stood thinking for a while, her eyes bright at the thought of action again. Nothing was more calculated to bring her to virile life than a challenge.

A faint sound behind her made her turn suddenly. She frowned, not observing anything different in the lounge. Then she saw that something had been added to the big polished table in the room's centre. It caught the incoming sunlight and reflected a myriad entrancing colours. Puzzled, she gazed down in wonder at a superbly wrought casket. But how it had got there was a mystery.

Picking it up, she turned it over and over in her hands, searching for the lock. She found it presently, a diamond stud inset into the basket's metal. The stud clicked under pressure, the lid flew up—then from the casket's interior there sprang something utterly incredible.

The Amazon jumped back as an object like a small snake fell to the carpet. She watched it in amazement. It was growing with tremendous rapidity, both in length and breadth. In perhaps a dozen seconds it was six feet long and six inches wide. There did not seem to be any distinct type of head, only a flattish extension of the main length with two vicious eyes, lidless and hypnotic.

The Amazon moved warily, and moving was the

very thing she ought not to have done. With bewildering speed the serpent flew at her, its coils lashing about her, pinning her arms to her sides. Immediately the coils began to tighten with a force such as she had never known. She began struggling frantically, realizing that here was something of demoniac strength. With every ounce of her strength she tried to force her arms away from her body and so tear free of that strangling grip, but even her supernormal muscles were useless. The thing went on tightening relentlessly, tiny needle-like suckers biting into her flesh. Close to her face the mouthless head with the boring eyes waved fantastically.

Gasping for breath, the Amazon reeled helplessly against the big table, then battered herself upon its edge in the hope that the blows would dislodge the reptile. It had not the slightest effect. It seemed to be steel-hard, and it went on still constricting. The Amazon lurched, her arms feeling as though they were being telescoped into her body, her lungs no longer able to function. She tried to shout, and had not the breath to do it. Choking, she toppled to the floor and made a last frantic effort to tear herself free. And again she failed. The coils felt like white-hot wire slowly cutting her on two. She lashed out with her feet and knocked over a tall ornamental stand; then she could do no more.

Her last effort brought Relka from the adjoining laboratory to investigate. He looked about him, then caught sight of the Amazon half unconscious on the floor, her face and neck purple, her tongue protruding.

She gave a quick, anguished movement of her glazing eyes toward the hideous thing that was breaking her in two—then the Jovian hurled himself forward.

Seizing the tail and head of the reptile, he extended his mighty arms with every vestige of his vast strength. And very slowly the inexorable coils had to loosen—until at last with a sudden jerk he had whirled the reptile free. Immediately he battered it with blinding force against the wall. When it had fallen to the floor he lifted the big oak table, swung it high over his head, then crashed it down on the squirming thing threshing on the carpet. It vanished under the ruined table. A small length of tail protruded. It quivered, then ceased moving.

Struggling for breath, her clothing ripped, her flesh feeling as if white-hot wire had been wrapped about it, the dishevelled Amazon struggled to her feet. For several seconds she could not speak. She motioned to Relka and he raised the remains of the table and tossed them aside. The snake was dead, apparently, part of it crushed.

"Where in cosmos did it come from?" The Amazon stared at it. "It was sent to me in that magnificent casket lying on the floor over there. It was on the table."

Relka reached down his scaly paw and picked up the reptile by the tail. He contemplated it, then his thoughts reached the Amazon as she rubbed her aching arms gently.

"This is an *estiron*, Amazon," he explained. "One of the most terrible serpents known to my world. It kills by sheer constrictive power. It doesn't live by atmo-sphere—otherwise this air of Earth would have killed it. It absorbs energy, stores it, and uses it as needed. It has the quality of evolving from birth to maturity at tremendous speed."

"So I noticed." The Amazon was still breathing hard. "It was no larger than a worm when it fell out of the casket: the next thing I knew it had flown at me."

"It attacks all living things and tries to absorb their energy."

The Amazon turned in disgust from the dead reptile and picked up the fallen casket from the floor. With it in her hands she went to the window and studied its exquisite workmanship.

"Would you say this came from your world too?" she asked Relka.

"Possibly. Certainly the snake did. This was a delib-erate attempt to kill you, Amazon, and had I not been close at hand it would have succeeded. It begins to look as though your theory about Sefner Quorne is not so far wrong. He must have sent that snake. But how did it get here?"

"It suddenly appeared—which suggests four-dimen-sional transit, in which Quorne is a master. As you say, it was an attempt to kill me, and only Quorne could be at the back of it." The Amazon frowned. "The only thing I do not understand is why he should try to bait me with hypnotic dreams on the one hand, and on the other try to kill me with a serpent. The two are difficult to reconcile."

"Possibly he believes you are not falling for his hypnotic bait, and so is trying to kill you by other means."

"Possibly," the Amazon admitted. "And he is either working from Jupiter with all the resources of the city which lies buried there under a broken dome, or else he is operating from Saturn, having had materials taken there. It would seem, though, since that thing is a Jovian snake, that he may be on the giant planet—which means I'm changing my plans. I am going to Jupiter first. If Quorne is not there, I shall go on to Saturn. He will find me only too ready to accept this challenge."

She put down the casket on the window ledge and started attending to the minor injuries the reptile had inflicted.

"I hope I may come with you, Amazon?" Relka asked, and she looked back over her shoulder as she reached the doorway.

"Of course. I cannot imagine myself without you, much less so on the world from which you came."

# CHAPTER TWO
## WRONG DECISION

An hour later the *Ultra* was on its way. The Amazon, clad in a close-fitting suit of black with a solid belt of gold about her waist, gazed intently through the port. Relka, taking on the job of navigator, and charting the fairly familiar course to Jupiter, stole a glance at her now and again. Her features were harshly set; a vindictive gleam lay in her violet eyes. He knew those signs. The fact that she had been nearly killed had resolved her to find Sefner Quorne this time, even if she travelled to the end of the universe to do it.

There was not room in the Solar System for both Sefner Quorne and the Golden Amazon. One or the other had to be obliterated.

"You could have reached Jupiter almost instantly by dissembly of atoms," Relka pointed out. "We could have rebuilt ourselves upon reaching the planet."

"Yes," the Amazon said, "but l may need weapons, therefore I must use this *Ultra* of mine. Time is of no particular consequence, as long as I succeed."

The Amazon was in a brittle mood. She left the control board once the course was determined, and fixed the automatic pilot in position. From here on it would be a matter of waiting and killing time until the asteroid region was reached: then would come the brief evading ceremony to avoid being smashed to pieces by hurtling cosmic rocks.

Ahead, Mars—outermost of the four inner planets—swelled until it filled all the void; then it was left behind and there remained the vast gap to Jupiter with the asteroid belt between.

Throughout most of the journey, since she slept but little at any time, the Amazon sat near the universal window, which gave a view on all parts of the cosmos. Several times Relka saw her there, a superb figure in her black tights, her chin resting on her yellow hand, her golden hair drawn to the back of her perfectly shaped head by a jewelled clasp. She seemed back in those moods of abstract thought, her eyes gazing into distance, a solemnity in her bearing that Relka, born of an alien world, found hard to understand.

Possibly no Earth being could have understood either. The Amazon was aware for the first time since the death of Abna that she really had no happiness in living without him.

When he had been alive she had scorned the thought of his being an essential part of her life. Now he was dead, she was ready to admit how mistaken she had been. But it had taken her a year of loneliness to discover it. She was a superwoman who had everything, and yet had nothing. Beauty, endless wealth, vast physical strength, scientific genius, the inhabitants of two worlds bowing down to her unobtrusive leader-ship—all these were hers, and yet were not enough. She could no longer find an interest in investigating and exploring for the sheer sake of it. Something had come into her life, and gone out again—and it had left an irreparable hurt.

Relka's advice that the asteroids were not far away broke her almost continuous mood of reminiscing. She moved from the universal window, guided the huge *Ultra* safely above the plane of the "minefield" of aster-oids, and then retired again to brood. There was still a long distance to go before Jupiter became a compelling gravity field.

Now and again, she found herself wondering why no further hypnosis seemed to affect her; then she decided it must be because Quorne had fully believed his grim trick with the Jovian snake had succeeded. On the other hand, he had instruments capable of showing exactly where she was, so it was queer he did not renew his attack on her mental stronghold. Whatever the answer, she was left more or less free, until within 10,000,000 miles of Jupiter. Then, just as that colossal gravity field was making itself felt, she found herself in the grip of ideas and thoughts which she was profoundly convinced were not her own.

She struggled hard against them as she sat at the control-board, gazing out on to the mighty face of Jupiter, his cloud-wreaths girt about him and whirling under the stupendous force of the hurricanes lashing his surface.

"Relka," she said at last, turning a strained face. "We are not going to Jupiter. We are going to Saturn."

His thoughts expressed astonishment. "But why, Amazon? I thought you were thoroughly decided that—"

"I have changed my mind. You'd better reset the course."

Relka did not argue, even though he did not understand. The Amazon passed a hand over her forehead, puzzled as to why it should ache so heavily. There was an oppression on her brain which she could not fathom, and the oppression seemed to take the form of an implacable command to go to Saturn and not Jupiter. She assumed it could only be Quorne at work with high-powered hypnotic amplifiers, against which she stood no chance.

No chance? A notion came to her. Getting up quickly, she moved to a panel and closed one of the switches. There was a brief grinding noise as radiation-proof plates rolled into position on the outside of the vessel, completely sealing it off from all known forms of radiation, including cosmic waves. Thought waves, when sent through an amplifier, had a similar wavelength to cosmic waves, so the plates ought to block the hypnosis—yet they did not. The ache and the command in her brain remained undimmed.

"It's a mystery," she declared, switching the plates out of commission again. "What kind of power can Quorne be using to be able to subject me even through insulation?"

"Quorne's science is known to be brilliant," Relka responded, for the sake of a better comment.

Completely baffled, the Amazon returned to her control chair and remained in it until she had swung the vessel clear of Jove's huge attraction. Fortunately, Saturn was on the same side of the sun as Jupiter at this time, so after a change of course, Saturn eventually came into view—its image greatly magnified on the viewing plate—a planet of incredible beauty, rings at an angle, shining with a deep yellow whiteness. The Amazon frowned to herself as she contemplated that beauteous world. She remembered the amethyst city and the mystery land of warm sunlight, dancing flowers and green fields; and she also remembered the real Saturn, with its deadly rocky landscape and poisonous atmosphere, comprised mainly of ammoniated hydrogen, on the principle of Jupiter.

Suddenly Relka's thoughts spoke with sudden urgency.

"Look, Amazon! A space machine!"

In surprise she turned from gazing at Saturn and looked back in the direction of distant Jupiter. A silver speck, becoming rapidly larger, was sweeping through space in fast pursuit of the *Ultra*.

"It looks like Quorne's machine!" the Amazon said in amazement. "But why should his hypnosis drive me away from Jupiter when he obviously could do better if I went there? I can't understand this situation at all—"

"He's gaining," Relka interrupted. "If you want to break free of him, you'd better put on speed."

The Amazon's mouth tightened. "All I wish to do is destroy him, Relka, not escape him—and this may be my chance. I wonder if he'll answer a radio call? I have to be sure whom I'm attacking."

She switched on the radio and spoke briefly into the microphone, identifying herself. She was interrupted in the middle of a sentence.

"I had hoped, Amazon, that you would come to Jupiter—but evidently you have not the courage. Which I find surprising! That being so, I intend to destroy you. Where you are heading I can only guess, but I assume it is Saturn. You are wasting your time. Saturn is a world of poison gas, hurricanes, and death. Or are you looking for that illusive amethyst city? I saw that delusion, as you must have, but I have never seen it since."

The Amazon did not have the chance to say any more, for Quorne cut her off. But at least she knew she was dealing with him. There was no mistaking that smooth, cultured voice.

"Stand by to attack, Relka." The Amazon glanced at the Jovian quickly. "I'll pilot the *Ultra* and you do the firing. Quorne must be crazy if he thinks that small machine of his can stand up against my weapons."

Knowing that Quorne was anything but crazy, however, the Amazon was prepared for any trick he might pull. She slowed the *Ultra* down, then swung it around to give Relka a better chance of using his weapons. He settled himself at the weapon control panel, fingers on the switches, his eyes fixed on the firing screen with its hair-thin demarcation lines.

Out of the gulf came Quorne, the size of his machine rapidly increasing. In the distance lay a scattering of Jupiter's numerous moons. Then suddenly an orange ray flashed across the gulf and struck the *Ultra* amidships. The Amazon smiled coldly, satisfied that the insulated metal could withstand anything Quorne wished to hurl at her. She was right. The beam, in the order of a heat ray, reflected back into space harmlessly.

"Let him have it!" she ordered, and Relka closed the switches on the *Ultra*'s most deadly weapon—the protonic cannon.

A livid pencil of disintegrative fire blasted straight at Quorne's machine. On the nose of it the plate buckled and began to roll up like charred paper, but by a masterful piece of space navigation he hurled the vessel to one side and dodged the frightful stream of energy. The Amazon scowled and began to manoeuvre the *Ultra* once again.

Quorne replied with lavender and green beams this time, one disintegrative and the other a freezing ray. Neither of them made any impression. Then came something else, stabbing up from Jupiter itself, through the cloudbanks. It was a beam that had the Amazon baffled. It was black, the most extraordinary thing she had ever seen. Too late she tried to swing the *Ultra* away. The segment of black whirled around, struck the *Ultra*, and sent it spinning madly like a top.

The effect in the control room was chaotic. Relka

was hurled backward from the weapon range, and the Amazon was pitched out of her chair and flung against the farther wall. Completely out of control, the *Ultra* began to fall back into the gravity of Jupiter.

The Amazon forced herself up from the floor and kept a hold of the wall struts to prevent herself from being flung over.

"That is negative force he's using," she panted. "That's why it's black. It doesn't disintegrate matter—it batters. He can fling the *Ultra* where he wants. Evidently his Jovian laboratory is working at full pressure again."

Clinging to the wall, she inched herself back to the control board. Outside, space seemed to be turning somersaults while the *Ultra* apparently remained still. Far below, Jupiter was gyrating and whirling crazily. Once down there in that vast gravity, surrounded by ammoniated hydrogen atmosphere, the Amazon knew she would be finished. Quorne would see to that. So she closed the switches and gave the rockets facing Jupiter all the power they possessed.

The effect slewed the *Ultra* away from the giant planet, but it immediately fell into an opposite attraction, this time from Ganymede, one of the larger moons. Too late, the Amazon saw her mistake and all her frantic efforts to pull free were useless. She was only 1,000 miles from the satellite and plunging at terrific speed.

Breathlessly she watched that crazy little landscape flying out of space to meet her. She gave the forward rockets full power to check her fall, but there was little they could do at such short notice. Within a few minutes, so fast was the *Ultra* dropping, the brief air depth of Ganymede screamed around the ship—then it crashed.

The Amazon was pitched helplessly across the control room by the impact. There was a twanging of shock-absorbing springs, a rending of metal projections, the explosion of disrupted plates, the hiss of shattered rocket tubes—then a dead quiet. The power plant had stopped.

Slowly the Amazon got to her feet and looked about her. The first thing she noticed was the lightness of the gravity. Relka also struggled up. Neither he nor the Amazon were hurt, thanks to the powerful shock absorbers.

Her face grim, the Amazon moved across to the control board and made a test of the power unit. It wheezed in a very odd fashion, its copper bar atom provider out of alignment. Outside the machine, clouds of smoke rose as vegetation was briefly incinerated by the smashed rocket tubes.

"Ditched!" the Amazon declared bitterly. "I don't think the *Ultra* has ever taken such a beating before—Just let me get my hands on Quorne!"

She clenched her fists and glared through the observation window upon Ganymede's landscape.

The vessel had landed in the midst of a riotous jungle of weird, genetically engineered plants, over which shone the varied lights of Jupiter, the sister moons and—infinitely far away—the sun.

"Did you say Ganymede?" Relka asked, joining the Amazon in her scrutiny.

"Yes. One of the larger moons which the Cosmic Engineers from Earth have started to modify at my instructions, so as to make it a possible future mining colony. Slight gravity, oxygen-hydrogen air up to two miles, lush vegetation specially created to help generate oxygen. On the same lines as Io—where I once ditched Abna. Maybe this is just retaliation. It's certainly not going to be a simple job to repair the *Ultra*. We'd better get outside and see what the damage is. We don't need space suits, because as well as created air there's a controlled release of heat from underground."

She turned to the airlock and unscrewed it. Pulling it open, she jumped lightly down into the under-growth and began wandering around the huge bulk of the almost upended vessel. Everywhere she and Relka looked they saw damage. The rocket tubes were completely shattered, several plates were no longer of use, and there were fissures in the outer casting.

"This job is going to take us several weeks," the Amazon decided finally, coming to a stop when the examination was complete. "But it's got to be done."

She paused and looked upward toward Ganymede's grey sky, her eyes narrowing. Against the backdrop of stars and attendant satellites an S of sparks was curving as a space flyer came swiftly down from the void.

"Quorne!" Relka said.

The Amazon said nothing, but her hand removed

her ray gun and she stood waiting. The space machine swept over the area where the *Ultra* lay, then it came back and settled nearby. The airlock opened and a slim, dark-headed man in the lilac-coloured clothing of a Jovian dignitary appeared. With his gun in his hand, he came through the undergrowth, followed by four other men. The Amazon waited, making no move.

When the Jovian scientist was close, his eyes, the colour of heliotrope, glanced over the battered *Ultra*.

"Rare for you to make a crash landing, Miss Brant," he commented.

"We can dispense with the fancy speeches, Quorne," she retorted, then she fired her ray gun.

Quorne remained as he was, grinning a little as the chest of his garment smoked into rags. Beneath it, a dully gleaming metal plate became visible.

"Precaution," he explained, and with a lightning movement he snatched the Amazon's gun from her. "Naturally, I would not have walked so boldly toward you had I not been protected."

"Negative energy and a chest shield," the Amazon snapped. "Both neat tricks, which upset my calculations. As a scientist, I congratulate you."

"Praise indeed," Quorne murmured, smiling acidly. "You will appreciate the fact, of course, that you cannot continue to upset my plans—"

"I was not aware you had any. For all I have known to the contrary—until now—you were dead."

"I gather my present of a Jovian reptile was something you did not feel able to accept?"

"Only as a challenge," the Amazon retorted. "Which I assume it was intended to be. I did not know even then that you were the sender, but it seemed a logical assumption. Like your hypnosis upon me for the past year."

A change of expression came to Quorne's thin, intellectual features.

"Hypnotism? I don't quite understand, Miss Brant."

She did not gratify him by explaining any further. A thought was turning over in her mind. She felt pretty sure from the Jovian scientist's manner that he was genuinely surprised; and if that were so, then who had created hypnotism?

"Naturally, I escaped Saturn," Quorne continued. "The dense cloud coverings helped me. After that I returned to my own planet—Jupiter. Then," Quorne nodded towards the four men with him, "I released the last remaining Atlantean men from the penal colony." He smiled faintly. "You did not quite succeed in your attempt to wipe out my race when you smashed the protective dome over our main city."

The Amazon frowned. She had completely forgotten about the small separate settlement, which Abna's father had created for banished criminals.

"Naturally they were grateful, and are loyal to me," Quorne continued. "Together we revived the science of Atlantis, and got the city to work again under its protective dome. Then I set out to accomplish the purpose for which I have so long striven—to break you, Miss Brant. The snake was a bait, yes, but I gather you lost your nerve at the last moment, since you turned away from Jupiter and headed for Saturn."

"I changed my plans."

"Change or otherwise, the answer is the same," Quorne commented. "First I am going to destroy this vessel of yours, then I am going to kill you and this Jovian who seems to have become so attached to you."

Quorne had forgotten for the moment that the Jovian had the power to read thoughts—hence Relka was warned in advance of what was intended.

Regardless of consequences, Relka dived forward, lashing up his scaled fist as he moved. It struck Quorne a glancing blow as he jerked his head sideways, but the next moment the scaly, vastly strong body had crashed into him and knocked him spinning. Immediately the four other men whipped around their ray guns. Two of them jabbed livid flame at the Jovian's scaly hide, but it had little effect: the other two found themselves grappling with the Golden Amazon, and being quite ordinary men, they felt as if they were fighting a tigress.

The Amazon's first dive in the light gravity brought her hands around the necks of the nearer two men. She smashed both men's heads together. They fell apart, half-senseless. Down came a yellow hand on the arm of the nearest man and a wrench snapped the bone viciously. He screamed, and it died in his throat as he was hurled a dozen yards and crashed unconscious into a rock.

Relka swung around, picked up the dazed Quorne in one hand, and then dashed him down to the ground again. Quorne gave a cry of anguish and grabbed at a gun within a foot of him. He fired blindly, the ray carving across the Amazon's left leg. She staggered, gritting her teeth with the pain as flesh charred to the bone, and the bone broke. Then she fell to the ground.

Relka's mailed fist crashed down on the head of the second man and flattened him to the ground. The third and fourth men swung their weapons around, but before they could fire them, that packed mass of super-muscle was plowing amidst them, battering at them with such force that bones broke under the blows.

Quorne, by no means unconscious, saw his chance. He fired, and the flame bit into the Jovian at the one vulnerable point—the unscaled portion across his midriff. He writhed desperately, then became still.

The Amazon lay as she had fallen, her face masked with pain.

Quorne got up and said: "I am wondering whether to fire a beam straight through your heart, Miss Brant, and finish you—or whether I should let you pass from the scheme of things more slowly. If I destroy your *Ultra*, you are powerless. You can lie here and die slowly in this lonely outpost of the spaceways."

"Do as you like," the Amazon whispered. "But if I die, Quorne, I'll come back from the farthest star to get you. If I live, I'll still get you."

"Perhaps we had better see which promise you can fulfil," Quorne suggested.

He went to his machine and from it there presently projected a disintegrator beam. It flashed to all parts of the already damaged *Ultra*, driving huge fissures in the massive plates, snapping off the remains of the rocket tubes, splintering the conning tower—and finally an extra savage burst sliced the nose of the vessel clean off and left half-molten, crumbled metalwork. The Amazon could not see the control room from her position, but she judged that it must be completely shattered, with the many connections essential to navigation melted into one common mass.

Satisfied, Quorne ceased his wrecking activities. He returned and, one by one, picked up his guards and carried them to his ship. Then he contemplated the Amazon from a distance.

"I am not leaving any men in case they happen to have some life in them," he said. "They might become sentimental enough to help you. As for Relka, your Jovian servant there, I fancy he will never return to life."

The Amazon was in too much pain to answer. She was doing her best to stem the flow of blood from the wound the ray had inflicted. When she heard the sound of rocket exhaust, she looked up. Quorne's machine was hurtling upward on its way back to Jupiter.

The Amazon passed her dry tongue over lips that were salty, and tried to think straight in the blur clouding her body and mind.

If she could reach the vessel, and the first aid equipment was still in existence, she had materials that could help her injury, if not cure it. So, setting her teeth, she forced herself up and stood on one leg. Then she began a series of hops—but within a few seconds, strong though she was, dizziness brought her down. She had lost so much blood she was rapidly weakening.

She wormed her body along until she gained the side of Relka. She caught at his outflung scaly paw and pulled at it.

"Relka!" she panted hoarsely. "Relka, help me—if you can!"

The fallen Jovian was silent. Reaching his shoulders, she pushed them up, the light gravity helping her. He tumbled over on his back, his torn body revealed, and it told the Amazon that Relka would never be her companion again.

"If I ever live through this, Quorne, I'll spend the rest of my life paying you back," the Amazon whispered, her pain-deadened eyes staring up at mighty Jove.

She relaxed, struggling for breath, her whole body feeling as if it were alternately bathed in fire and water. The sweat of pain had soddened her close-fitting suit; it trickled down her drawn face. Then lights began exploding behind her eyes, and her last effort to fight off unconsciousness was unavailing.

The Amazon went down into a blackness where pain and awareness no longer existed.

# CHAPTER THREE
## STRANGE HELPER

Out of the drifting abyss, the tops of trees began to form before the Amazon's returning vision. There were sounds. The soft whisper of the newly-created winds of Ganymede, the eternal rustle of the strange trees, a sound like the contact of metal instruments against each other. And a drowsy peace. She was warm, without pain, and with strength coming back to her.

She looked about her. At first she could not be sure but what she was gazing at an illusion. For the *Ultra* was almost completely repaired and, assisting in the control of a powerful atomic-welding apparatus was Relka! His midriff, which had been so savagely blasted, was normal again.

Even more baffling was the presence of a young woman in maroon slacks and orange-coloured blouse, working with the Jovian with the welder. She was slim of build and probably looked to be nineteen or twenty, with the most extraordinary shade of hair. It was copper-bronze, but so silken it reflected light from its waves as it tumbled unchecked to her slender shoulders. Her exposed skin was almost the same colour as her hair, having a decided sheen. Her features the Amazon could not see, as she was turned away toward the ship.

Feeling her strength had completely renewed itself, the Amazon looked at her shattered leg. Her gaze fixed on it incredulously. It was perfectly normal, though the rent in her black tights showed that the injury had been there. Carefully she examined the spot, but could find no trace of where the wound had been.

She frowned. She remembered only one person who had ever had the power to master matter so completely that it obeyed a mental order. That person had been Abna—and he was dead. Or perhaps—?

The Amazon got to her feet quickly, excited at the thought that perhaps Abna, the Lord of Jove, had actually returned from the dead and restored her and Relka. He might even be working at the other side of the *Ultra*.

She hurried over to the giant machine, and the strange girl and Relka turned at her advance. The Jovian could not express any emotion by his features, but the Amazon was under no doubt regarding the warm thankfulness of his thoughts. His scaly hands grasped hers tightly in friendship as she came up, and for a second or two the yellow eyes were almost human.

"You are well again, Amazon," his thoughts said. "Even as I am. It is all the more wonderful in my case because I was dead."

Blankly the Amazon looked beyond him to the girl.

She was good-looking beyond the average. Her nose was straight and exactly the right length. The chin was firm but still feminine. It was the mouth and the eyes that attracted the Amazon most. The lips were full and parted in the merriest smile she had ever seen, like that of a child with no responsibilities. Her eyes had complete frankness and high intelligence—starry, dancing, and blue as the rarest sapphires.

"I suppose I should thank you for everything that has happened?" the Amazon asked in wonder.

"For fixing you up, you mean?" The girl's merry smile changed to a laugh and revealed perfect rows of snowy teeth. "Oh, that's all right. Anything to oblige. You were in a pretty sorry mess, you know."

The Amazon still gazed in wonder. "I was nearly dead from a shattered leg, and my companion here *was* dead. Yet now—" She spread her hands helplessly.

"I soon fixed you up," the girl said, as though nothing of great importance had been achieved. "And I think you'll find your spaceship is all right again, too. A good deal of welding was needed, and the controls were in a terrible mix. I managed to sort them out and built in a new panel."

"You sorted them out?" The Amazon's bewilderment was complete. "But how? It took me three years to work out that control board and—"

"You went the long way round," the girl explained, and her infectious smile returned. "You'll find I've made things less complicated, but just as efficient." She nodded to the nearby plates of the machine. "Relka and I have just these last plates to flow into union, then the ship will be about as good as new."

The Amazon looked at the machine, at Relka, and then the smiling girl. She took hold of her slim young shoulders in her yellow hands.

"Who are you?" she asked, puzzled. "From your appearance you are a girl of Earth, yet from your amazing knowledge and intelligence— Well, I just don't know. You're a mystery."

"Mystery?" The girl threw back her head with its extraordinary copper-bronze hair and laughed. "Not I. I'm just a space traveller enjoying myself. My name is Viona," she added, as if in an afterthought.

"Viona what?" the Amazon questioned.

"Just Viona. I rather like my name. It's musical, don't you think?"

With that the girl withdrew and continued her work.

The Amazon, her brows knitted, surveyed the young figure from the back. It was still not thoroughly developed—not very broad on the shoulder, still boyish on the hips. In fact, Viona was a baffling problem—and the Amazon did not like a problem she could not solve.

The Amazon took the girl's arm firmly.

"Just a minute, Viona: I haven't nearly finished questioning you."

"Then come over to my space machine," the girl suggested. "There it is."

She nodded to a small neat ship and began walking toward it. The Amazon followed her. In another five minutes they were both settled at a meal of concentrates and essences.

"Do you come from Earth?" the Amazon questioned.

Viona shrugged. "I don't claim any particular planet as my birthplace. I wander about—and always have as long as I can remember."

"But you can't be more than twenty!"

"I suppose not," Viona reflected, her brilliant blue eyes far away from a moment. Then she laughed. "What does it matter? I enjoy living. It can be wonderful fun when you make matter obey you. It leaves nothing to be afraid of."

"I never quite achieved that sublime state of mind," the Amazon replied, still vaguely incredulous.

"I don't think one does achieve it," Viona commented, after a pause. "You're born with it—like a good voice, a great musical talent, or gigantic strength."

"But can't you tell me more about yourself? Who are your parents? Which planet do they live on?"

"It sounds silly, but I'm not sure."

The Amazon gave it up. Knowing what she did of the void, she was none too sure that this apparently laughing girl with the taking ways was not really some kind of synthetic decoy, perhaps being operated by Sefner Quorne. With even flesh and blood at his command, Quorne might do anything—then that seemed a foolish conception. Why should Quorne create an image that would restore the Amazon to health and bring Relka back from the dead?

"Worried, Amazon?" Viona asked presently.

"Not exactly that—baffled. I am wondering how

you ever happened to find me."

"I just happened to be cruising in this region, and I saw through my telescope that a wrecked space machine was lying here, so I descended to investigate."

"And you put me to rights again by mind force? Is that what I am supposed to believe?"

"Can you imagine any other force that could have done it?" And there was a fascinating twinkle in the sapphire eyes.

"And where are you going now?" the Amazon inquired.

"Earth, perhaps. Just as the mood seizes me...." Viona got to her feet and cleared away the remains of the concentrates. "I should think your *Ultra* ought to be finished now, and your friend Relka will need a meal. I have a special lot of ammonia crystals I know he'll relish."

The Amazon was too lost in thought to respond. The girl moved to the airlock, hailed Relka, and in a moment or two he had come into the control room. He had a meal of his own poisonous variety, using nitric acid as drink. Then when it was over his yellow eyes strayed from Viona to the meditating Amazon.

"I read profound doubt and wonder in your thoughts, Amazon," he remarked, and she gave a wry smile.

"Is that so extraordinary, considering this young space traveller here. She has rare beauty, far-reaching intelligence, and claims the mastery of her mind over matter. Do you realize that makes me seem—amateurish?"

"I don't agree with that," Viona said. "I don't bother using my gifts: I just have them and accept them as being as natural as breathing. You, on the other hand, use your powers for the general good of mankind, even if there was once a time when you didn't."

The Amazon's violet eyes sharpened. "How do you know about that?"

"All history recorders have noted the fact. Is it so strange I should know of it?"

The Amazon got to her feet, musing. Then she asked, "Do you come from Saturn, Viona?"

"Why do you ask?"

"Because there is something strange about Saturn. It has an earthly-looking paradise amid its poison vapours and lonely reaches. I saw it once—an amethyst-coloured city. I could imagine a young woman as lovely and carefree as you coming from such a place."

"Many worlds are my resting place," Viona said. Then after a pause she added, "And I must be on my way. I have done my job as far as you are concerned, Amazon, and I have really enjoyed meeting you—and faithful Relka."

The Amazon was not quite sure whether or not she was being ordered out, but in any event she stepped through the open airlock, Relka following her. They both looked back at the slim, smiling girl in the circular opening.

"Best of luck," she said, waving her hand in fare-well. "Especially against Sefner Quorne."

Then the airlock had closed and the Amazon gave

Relka a puzzled glance,

"How did she know about Quorne? Did you tell her?"

"No, Amazon. I would rather poison myself than mention his name."

The Amazon was silent again, wondering, her eyes following Viona's tiny but incredibly swift space machine as it darted away into the Ganymedian sky.

"Few problems have ever caused me such thought," the Amazon declared, turning. "However, I imagine the contemplation of a young woman with unusual powers is something I can dwell upon in leisure moments: our task now is to deal with Sefner Quorne. To destroy him."

"And as quickly as possible," Relka confirmed. "We have the advantage because he believes us dead."

"Advantage or otherwise, we're risking striking at him on Jove there," the Amazon declared. Then she moved toward the *Ultra*, the mystery of a young woman with copper-bronze hair thrust to the back of her mind.

On Jupiter, safe within the city under its protective dome which sealed off the poisonous ammoniated-hydrogen atmosphere, Sefner Quorne was deep in plans with his associates.

There were no more than 100 men on Jove, and women none at all. The city under the dome was an exact duplicate of Atlantis. Quorne was a descendant of the Atlanteans—with all the skill his heritage conferred. Abna had been the chosen ruler until his death. The history of the city went back to the Deluge of Earth, when an extra-terrestrial cataclysm had led the prescient Atlanteans to fly to Jove to avert catastrophe. Now, with Abna dead, Quorne was unchallenged ruler. And he still had his dream—and the scientific machinery to make it come true—the dream of conquering the whole universe and bringing it under Atlantean domination. With the Golden Amazon, his mortal enemy, dead, there was nothing to stop him.

He was in the controlling office of the enormous building that was the headquarters of Atlantis. Around him were master scientists, the few who believed with him that the universe could be bent to their genius. Among these was Nilfon, Quorne's chief assistant.

"The way is clear, my friends," Quorne said, looking about him on the intent faces gathered round the polished table. "The Golden Amazon is dead—or if not that, she soon will be. Her death will be lingering, which I regard as justifiable. The moment that aura needle flickers to zero, her life is extinct."

The scientists looked across at a nearby table. In the middle of it stood a transparent globe on a metal base. In the globe's centre, a diamond-tipped needle was poised on a delicate mechanism to an angle of forty-five degrees, pointing directly to the position of the moon Ganymede. The needle was attuned to the exact aura-energy given off by the Amazon—or any living organism—and as such was an infallible guide to her position.

"She clings to life a long time, Quorne," Nilfon

remarked. "It is over three hours since you returned from Ganymede and she is not dead yet."

"She will be," Quorne replied confidently. "In the meantime we have plans to lay. Having failed so far in direct attack on the inner planets, which must be the first to fall under our sway, I have decided on other methods. We can accomplish our purpose by bringing to ruin the cities of Earth and Mars. We are small in numbers if mighty in science, so the more we can do without exposing ourselves to danger, the better."

"Agreed," one of the scientists murmured. "What have you in mind, Excellency?"

"Rust," Quorne answered.

The scientists glanced at one another in surprise; then Quorne began to elaborate.

"Rust! Rust can break up the mightiest civilization that ever existed. It can destroy everything the Amazon has built up. The cities of Earth and newly reborn Mars can be corroded until they fall apart. When that happens, and the people are demoralized in consequence, we have nothing to do but step in and take control."

"And you believe that the metals being used on the inner planets are capable of being rusted?" Nilfon asked.

"It will take ages," another scientist remarked.

"Normally, yes," Quorne agreed. "But if the atmosphere of the two planets became impregnated with a metallic corrosive—which I have devised—that saturates all metal constantly, there is nothing to prevent everything of metal breaking up within six months. I call this corrosive nitrine. As for its power—well, see for yourself."

Quorne signalled a guard standing by the door, and evidently knowing in advance what was required of him, he departed into the adjoining laboratory. He reappeared with a block of metal about two inches squared, and pushed before him an atomiser-device on a rubber-wheeled trolley.

Putting the metal cube on a protective sheet on the table, Quorne said: "This metal is a combination of tungsten, iron-x, and mandanite, three of the toughest metals known to science, of which most cities and machines are composed. Now observe this."

He switched on the atomizer, directing the nozzle downward toward the cube. A fine, iridescent spray hovered in the bright artificial light, descending upon the cube. Almost immediately it changed colour. From grey it became brown, then red. It appeared to contract, flaking away in leaf-thin sheets that became powder. In about five minutes nothing remained of the cube except a heap of reddish-brown dust.

Quorne looked at his fascinated colleagues and gave his thin smile.

"A silent but relentless destroyer," he explained. "My proposition is to fire to the two inner planets a series of projectiles—an unending stream of them, in fact—which will explode as they strike the upper atmosphere of those worlds. Their disintegration will never be seen at that height. They will release their contents—this nitrine fluid—and by its own weight and carried by wind currents it will descend to the surface. Nobody will notice the stuff. It can be breathed or swallowed without harm—but in a very short time, the impregnation of the stuff in the atmosphere will rot metal everywhere—so rapidly that nobody will be able to stop it. I, of course, have the antidote—and I shall retain it until it is needed. Those whom we are determined to master will fight an invisible foe. When their cities and weapons and space ships are destroyed, we shall take over."

"And there is enough of this nitrine to deal with both planets?" Nilfon asked.

"Since its basis is water, it is inexhaustible."

"Excellent work," one of the scientists commented. "The sooner you launch, the scheme the better."

"The first loaded projectiles can begin their journeys to Earth and Mars within an hour; and after that a constant procession of them will keep up the attack."

"Just the same, Earthlings are not fools," Nilfon said. "Don't let's make the mistake of underestimating them. Even without the help of the Golden Amazon, they know many scientific tricks. They will be bound to suspect an external cause for the corrosion—then we'll have a fleet of space ships coming this way. They'll guess that no other planet can be the source of their troubles."

"The space machine that can defeat our weapons has not been created," Quorne retorted. "Not even by the Amazon. We'll very easily deal with whatever trouble there happens to be—" He glanced up sharply as a scientist entered. "Yes, what is it?"

"I'm reporting from the observatory, Excellency—the chief astronomer told me to inform you that an unidentified space machine has been seen leaving Ganymede. It is now moving in the direction of the Asteroid Belt, and Earth is the probable destination. Or else Mars."

Quorne looked amazed for a moment. "Space machine in this region? But it's incredible. I must see for myself."

He hurried to the observatory. Here the complicated telescopic devices were at work, utilizing the power of x-rays to penetrate the cloudbanks. Along magnetic beams light-photons were travelling, drawn from the void itself, and reflecting onto a twenty-foot-diameter mirror sunk in the floor. Quorne gripped the handrail around the mirror, and gazed fixedly at a tiny space ship hurtling through the void.

"It is moving at a tremendous velocity, Excellency," the chief astronomer remarked. "About half the speed of light, which is phenomenal. Our fastest space fliers cannot approach that."

"I'm not interested in the scientific velocity of this flyer," Quorne snapped. "I want to know who he is—and what he's doing. Try to contact him by radio."

"I did try, Excellency. There was no response."

Quorne tightened his grip on the rail, his eyes glinting. Already the speck of a space machine was becoming remote. In sudden anger he turned away and in a few moments had regained the controlling office.

"I don't like the situation," he said bitterly. "An unidentified space machine in this region is extremely disturbing, and it's moving faster than any flyer ever moved before except for the Amazon's craft. It surely can't be the Amazon because—"

He stopped, staring at the aura-compass. The needle, instead of having sunk to zero by this time, was pointing directly upward instead, and moving slightly.

"Apparently the Amazon is not dead," Nilfon commented, with a grim look. "From the look of this aura-compass she is in space somewhere—and moving."

"Come!" Quorne snapped. "We had better take a look from the observatory."

Once be reached it again, he gave curt orders. The telescopic equipment was swung round on its huge universal mountings and on the screen there presently appeared a vision of the *Ultra*, sailing majestically against the disc of Ganymede and becoming slowly larger.

The shock to Quorne's complacency was considerable, especially after having seen the other unidentified spaceship.

"It's incredible!" he declared blankly. "I smashed the *Ultra* beyond repair, and I am convinced the Amazon herself was sufficiently injured to die. Yet here is her ship, and if the aura-compass is right, which it must be, she is controlling it."

"Which means," Nilfon said, shrugging, "that

whoever was in that other spaceship must have performed some magical feats of surgery and engineering."

Quorne reflected, then came to a decision.

"Whatever the side issues, the fact remains that the Amazon is headed this way—and she will have such a welcome as she has never known. We'll prepare the weapon range immediately. If by any chance she should dodge the onslaught we'll hurl at her, then we'll pursue her into space. I don't pretend to understand yet why my plans have gone wrong, but I do know she can't get away with it. She'll be a little time yet getting here, so in the interval the first nitrine-fluid projectiles can be fired to the inner planets."

# CHAPTER FOUR
## A TRANSFORMATION

Seated at the *Ultra*'s control board, watching the giant globe of Jupiter coming ever nearer, the Amazon was lost in thought. It was one of those periods when there was nothing to do but wait for the journey to be over—and also keep a lookout for danger—so she had the chance to go back over some of the things that were puzzling her.

Viona was one puzzle, but there was also another. Sefner Quorne had said that he was not responsible for the hypnosis of the past year—so somebody else must be. Quorne's bait had not been hypnosis, but a deadly serpent. It left the mystery of the hypnosis deeper than ever. And the only conceivable answer was an impossible one—from the Amazon's point of view, anyway. As far as she knew, no person could send hypnosis across space except Quorne, by scientific methods; or Abna, by resources peculiarly his own. Yet Abna was dead.

Then she turned her attention to trying to devise a plan whereby she could approach Jupiter without detection. She knew that the Jovian telescopes had probably already picked her up, but there was an answer to that. She closed a switch, and immediately a polarizing shield covered the ship's exterior, bending the light waves reflecting from it. Thereby, to an onlooker the *Ultra* became invisible.

"Relka, I think we—" The Amazon half turned to him, to begin an outline of her plan, then she hesitated and relaxed a little in her chair. For the life of her she could not remember what she had been intending to say.

"Yes?" came Relka's telepathic inquiry, as he came over to her.

"It doesn't matter," she said after a moment. "I've changed my plan. I'm not dealing with Quorne just yet: I must go to Saturn first."

"But, Amazon, that's exactly what happened before! You were within an ace of reaching Jupiter and then you detoured for Saturn—and were brought down on Ganymede."

"I know. I don't understand myself, Relka, so don't ask for explanations. All I know is: I must go to Saturn."

She could not explain the decision even to herself, possessing as she did such a devouring hatred for Quorne. She turned the *Ultra*'s nose slowly around and then headed away from Jupiter as fast as his massive drag would permit. She took care to leave on the polarizing shield in the hope that invisibility would defeat the scientists of Jove who were doubtless waiting for her. But she had forgotten that an aura compass was probably turned on her.

In fact she had forgotten everything save that she must go to Saturn. And with constantly increasing speed the *Ultra* shot beyond the orbits of Jupiter's moons and carried on with ever-mounting speed into the gulf of space. Thousands of miles were eaten up. The thousands became millions, until at last the Amazon cut out the acceleration and maintained a constant velocity. With the course set on the ringed planet, she and Relka could relax for a while.

They did so for given intervals, one in charge while the other slept or ate. Then Relka, intently watching the shrinking globe of Jupiter through the telescopic sights, saw four infinitesimal specks far away. He looked across at the Amazon, who lay relaxed on the wall bed.

"We're being pursued, Amazon," came his thoughts. "We may be invisible, but there's evidently some way to detect us."

She got up from the bed and came to look through the lenses.

She said: "They're a tremendous distance away, and I can still get more speed out of the *Ultra* and will. Once we have got to Saturn, we'll probably lose them."

"You won't explain why you insist on going to Saturn, I suppose?"

"I can't. I don't know myself. It's just—an urge. Now, prepare for some strong acceleration."

She went to the control board and began to build up more power, and then more again. With her perfectly attuned body she was able to stand the strain, even though she felt like a block of lead for weight. Relka had infinite physical resistance inherited from life on Jupiter with his crushing gravity field. At breathtaking speed the *Ultra* licked up the millions of miles still yawning before Saturn could come within measurable distance, and in the remote distance the pursuing machines became smaller and smaller, unable to achieve the vastly greater speed of the *Ultra*.

Six more hours of this terrific velocity brought Saturn to filling all the void, an amazing and majestic world with his superb ring formation. Saturn was a dangerous planet to approach. The rings, being made up of multi-millions of small moons and planetoids, comprised a veritable "minefield" with their opposing attractions and narrow spaces, and the Amazon had to slow down as the outermost edge of the rings was reached. Thereafter she was not absent from the controls for a single moment, using the repulsive screen to turn aside the "hailstorm" of whirling rocks.

For over an hour she nosed the machine through the danger area, which covered 12,000 miles, then for a spell there was comparative peace as the 1,800-mile gap of Cassini's Division—the gap between rings— was covered. And so through the 17,000 miles of further rocks and planetoids, and out of that again into space with the surface of Saturn, covered in whirling cloud belts, lying 8,000 miles below.

Definitely Saturn was not an easy world to reach in safety, nor was there much chance of approaching it from the angle whereby the rings did not interfere, for the gravity stresses they created were as dangerous as the planetoids themselves.

The Amazon looked intently at the cloud-belted scene below, becoming ever mightier and shaded to dull grey in the light of the far-flung sun, then she switched on the infra-screens in readiness for the plunge into the vapours. She did not know where she was heading: for all she knew was she must go to Saturn. And here she was.

The *Ultra* rapidly jumped the 8,000 miles and vanished in the clouds. Outside the observation windows there was nothing but the clinging reek of ammoniated hydrogen, condensing on the proofed glass in glistening drops. As they went lower the atmosphere became so dense that it was almost liquid, but finally as they went lower in the screens the view was that of rocky landscape, twilight in tone, and utterly deserted.

"I cannot understand what you hope to achieve by this, Amazon," Relka declared, his thoughts irritated. "This is an utterly dead, poisonous world. Poisonous to you, anyway, if not to me. What do you hope to find?"

She shrugged. "No idea. I just feel I'd like to look around, that's all."

Relka gave it up and the Amazon brought the vessel quickly below the cloudbanks, and settled it on a rocky plateau. Then she stopped the power plant, snapped off the invisibility, and stood looking through the observation port. It was the most cheerless sight that could be imagined. In many ways the Saturnian landscape was similar to that of Jupiter, but with certain exceptions. Saturn, with his less tightly packed materials, had a gravitational field far below that of Jove, and in consequence mountains had risen to normal heights. They loomed in the distance. In the foreground was the plain, and it seemed to extend on all sides for an interminable distance. Here and there the gaunt, sharp-edged rock was broken by stretches of thick, greenish-yellow mud, indicating the intense poison in the atmosphere.

"I think we'll explore," the Amazon said at length, and looked at Relka somewhat woodenly.

"In this vessel?" he questioned.

"No—on foot. I'll need a spacesuit. You'll be all right."

The Amazon turned to the storage cupboard, selected a suit, and then clambered into it. Within ten minutes she and Relka were fully armed and provisioned and the airlock was opened. Together they stepped out into the thin green fog that was the Saturnian atmosphere.

"Since everything is visible within our range on foot, I cannot see the point of exploring," came the Jovian's thoughts, and the Amazon answered him through her audiophone.

"Neither can I. I just feel that I must."

So, side by side, they began walking forward. The cloud overhead whirled and swung with terrific speed, driven by hurricane winds, which however seemed to be entirely confined to the upper limits—for down on the plain there was not even a breeze to disturb the bilious-looking liquid gas which lay in the rocks and mud-holes.

"Gravity is similar to Earth's," the Amazon remarked. "Saturn's interior must be— Look!" she broke off suddenly, and halted.

Relka paused too, and immediately his scaly paw closed over his gun. He yanked it from his belt. The Amazon too, weapon in her hand, stood waiting and feeling utterly unprotected, for the *Ultra* was a mile and a half distant.

Out of the cloud banks there had appeared four fast space machines, evidently the four that had been in pursuit from Jupiter. There was little doubt Quorne was in charge, a fact that was established when lethal beams began to project dangerously from the machines, slashing at the rocks below.

"We can't fight these!" the Amazon cried through her audiophone. "Take shelter—if you can!"

She began running, but there was no shelter to which she could escape. Only the unending rock, and none of it with a ledge under which there might have been protection. So there began instead a kind of hide-and-seek as Quorne and his three companion vessels rained down everything they possessed from beams to bombs. It kept the Amazon and Relka constantly on the run, dodging, throwing themselves flat, being knocked over by blast, but somehow they kept avoiding catastrophe.

But the Amazon knew it could not last. She also knew that Quorne could have wiped her and Relka out long ago had he wished; this was just amusement as far as he was concerned, until he chose to deal the blow that would mean the end. And it looked like coming now. The Amazon, exhausted from her efforts in the stifling spacesuit, saw one of the machines skimming not fifty feet above her, its disintegrator beam gouging out rock in a straight line as a plough turns soil. She tried to run away from it, tripped, and went stumbling straight in the ray's track. Instantly Relka hurtled over to her and seized her, struggling to drag her up, although he realized there was no chance.

But something happened. Within inches of them the ray faded out mysteriously. Not only that, but the ships themselves vanished. A strange golden light began to suffuse everything, and the hard rocks melted into soft grass. Utterly astounded, the Amazon and Relka slowly stood upright, absorbing the incredible scene.

They were no longer on a rocky plain in danger of death, with whirling green clouds overhead. They were in a field greener than anything Earth could offer. It seemed to be on the side of a gently sloping valley. In the valley, where there was no sign of habitation, were the silver threads of rivers, the deeper green of hedges, the yellow of what appeared to be cornfields. And the sky had become inexplicably blue. In the midst of it hung an amber-coloured ball of flame, invisibly supported, shedding its warmth and light down on this wonderland.

"It is it," the Amazon whispered through the audio-phone. "Relka, this is the land we saw before—the land of beauty, and peace...."

As her suit became intolerably hot at the rise in

temperature, she lifted off her helmet and stepped out of the clumsy coverings, putting them over her arm. Relka, able to breathe either oxygen or hydrogen, methane and ammonia, was in no wise incommoded. His scales too made him impervious to temperature changes.

"You took a risk, Amazon," he said. "The air might still have been poisonous to you."

She shook her head. "Not here, Relka. This is a little slice of Earth—utterly unexplained, yet so very, very beautiful. I wonder what became of our attackers? Oh, if only I could understand this riddle!"

She looked about her helplessly and the Jovian transmitted a sober thought.

"Beautiful it may be, but where is the *Ultra*? My compass was trained on its magnetic prow; now it's no longer working. What about yours?"

The Amazon glanced at the compass on her wrist. The needle was swinging aimlessly.

"Whoever or whatever produced this, and saved us from Quorne's murderous attack, can surely find the *Ultra* for us," she declared.

"Yes—unless the *Ultra* is in Quorne's field of activity and he destroys it." Relka looked about him with his yellow eyes and for once exerted his scientific capacity. "I think this is a segment of the fourth dimension," he said. "It has been swung through hyperspace by some tremendous force, and we were caught up in it. It is not the real Saturn, but a projection of a plane existing parallel to it."

The Amazon did not seem to be listening. She was gazing fixedly into distance, and at last she pointed.

"The amethyst city!" she cried. "There it is!"

Relka looked. That city had not been there a few minutes before; he was sure of it. But it was now, gleaming an iridescent purple in the golden light, its slender towers reaching to the serene blue sky. It looked just as it had done during that other brief glimpse of it over a year before. Its terraces and flower gardens were just the same. It was a thing of beauty beyond price.

"Now's our chance," the Amazon decided. "If it is an illusion, we'll prove it this time."

And she began hurrying through the grass towards that wondrous vision perched like a precious jewel on rising ground, perhaps three miles away. Relka kept beside her, moving rhythmically on his block-like legs, his yellow eyes fixed on the vision.

"No sign of life," he commented, "which is the one thing I don't understand. One would expect to find such a city teeming with people—lovely people, perhaps, from your standard of beauty, Amazon, if not from mine. But there is nothing."

The Amazon did not comment: she found his thoughts distracting. There was upon her once again the feeling that somewhere in this inexplicable city she might find Abna. She hurried her pace, fearing the vision would fade.

But the city was still substantial when she and Relka gained its outermost limits. They found that the soft green grass merged into the deep amethyst colour of the metal main street without a trace of where the joint came. Absorbed by the wonder of it all, they moved slowly along the vista, contemplating the delicate purple buildings, the terraces, the flowers.

The buildings were graceful and every one circular, each with a tapered spire on its summit. Doors were wide open. There were window spaces, but none had glass in them. Not a soul was in sight. The whole thing was as apart from the poisonous barren surface of the real Saturn as anything that could be conjectured.

"Pretty big building there," Relka said at length, nodding to it when they had reached the midway point of the street. "Might see what it contains."

With a nod the Amazon followed him up the broad, gleaming steps, and they passed through a cool, immaculate hall and into an enormous area lighted with a white brilliance that seemed somehow to be created by the walls themselves.

The source of the illumination puzzled them—until Relka made a guess.

"Some metals emit radiations, which, while not visible as light itself, have the same effect on the eye. This metal might be in that category."

The Amazon did not answer. She was gazing at a breathtaking sight. The enormous room, so completely deserted, was some kind of treasure-trove.

In tall cairns at different points on the immense floor were stones that caught the light in flashing rays. The Amazon hurried to the first pyramid and plunged her hand into it. Liquid blue fire seemed to surge and ripple around her hand, as the pyramid slipped. Tens of thousands of gems streamed down and tumbled about the floor.

"They're pure sapphires!" she cried, as Relka looked on. "Wealth beyond all imagination, in Earth values. And look—those there are rubies, I'm sure."

She hurried to the next pyramid, which gleamed with the hue of port wine. This time it was red fire that flowed around her eager hands as precious rubies flooded through her fingers. So she went on, to each tall pile in turn. There were diamonds, emeralds, opals, every conceivable jewel, and so many thousands of all of them that they dazzled the imagination. Deep in her heart the Golden Amazon was yet a woman, and she was looking on paradise. To the Jovian, stolid male of an alien world, the stones were simply chemical creations.

"Wealth, to such as you, Amazon, is useless," he commented.

"True, but whoever left them here wanted to please me. That is my guess. But what else is there?" She broke off quickly. "In that room over there—"

She went quickly across to the nearby open doorway, and entered what was plainly a powerhouse, lighted with the now familiar white glow. But all the immense generators, turbines, and other electrical equipment were silent.

Struck by an incredulous thought, the Amazon inspected the nearest enormous dynamo. It was yellow and immaculately clean. Then she looked at the other products of super-engineering. Relka came and joined her, surveying the high roof.

"Relka, this is beyond understanding," the Amazon said at last, her violet eyes expressing the utter perplexity that had overcome her. "These machines are of solid gold!"

"For which reason they should function better than any machines ever did," he answered.

"Yes—but gold! It's impossible! A powerhouse of this size, containing nothing but solid gold equip-ment—"

"If you would care for a meal, Miss Brant—and, of course, your friend—it is prepared for you."

A calm, cultured voice suddenly speaking in the vastness made the Amazon swing around in amaze-ment. Relka gazed with her at a man standing in the doorway. He was tall, blond, handsome, dressed in a sleeveless silken blouse and short trunks. His shoes were some kind of synthetic material and deadened his footfalls as he advanced.

"Then—then this place is not deserted!" the Amazon cried.

"That depends, Miss Brant, on how you look at it." There was an evasive humour about the man, an impish look in his blue eyes as he studied her. "However, if you will both come this way—"

"Before we do," the Amazon interrupted, "who are you, and what is this place? This city? How does it come to be on a world like this?"

"Why not on this world as much as any other? There

is no barrier to materialized thought waves. As for my name, it is Crinz. The city is called Millennia, a product of untold cycles of scientific refinement."

Crinz motioned deferentially to a doorway and moved toward it. For a moment the Amazon hesitated, then she began to follow, with Relka behind her.

They traversed the cool length of a gleaming corridor outside, turning off presently into a serenely lighted room where a sumptuous meal had been laid on a highly polished table.

The room was in the finest artistic taste. Everything about it spoke of untold wealth. The hangings were cloth-of-gold, the rugs perfectly matched skins. The furniture was extremely modern and of the finest quality. Quite convinced by now that she was in the midst of a dream, the Amazon seated herself at the table and considered the fare. There were no essences and restoratives—the usual food of a space traveller— but a genuine meal of fowl, fish, and meat, while wine stood nearby. The cutlery was solid gold. In a cut glass dish stood a tall heap of ammonia crystals, Relka's favourite food; and next to it a flagon of nitric acid for his especial use.

"Please partake of whatever you wish, Miss Brant," the handsome servant invited, then stood with folded arms, ready to be attentive to the smallest wish.

Since she was both hungry and thirsty, the Amazon did not hesitate; but she also made it the opportunity to ask questions.

"How do you know my name, Crinz?"

"I know all things," Crinz responded. "That is inevitable when matter is ruled by thought."

"I have heard somebody else make that statement recently," the Amazon mused. "A young woman by the name of Viona. Do you know her?"

"No, Miss Brant. I never heard the name—"

The servant paused, his handsome face inscrutable, as his sentence was suddenly interrupted by laughter. It was masculine and deep, and the most rollicking laugh the Amazon had ever heard. She looked around in amazement.

"Who is that?" she asked, but Crinz only raised and lowered his shoulders.

The laughter came again, peal upon peal of it, yet it had a queer disembodied quality and seemed to pass through the walls. It spoke of a personality rich in fun, of one enjoying a tremendous joke. The Amazon's expression changed and she got to her feet.

"I resent being laughed at!" she snapped.

The laughter died away. Then as the quietness returned, she relaxed a little and sat down again.

"Perhaps I was a little hasty," she admitted. "I suppose it is all part of the mystery of this place."

She resumed her meal, realizing that if she ever wished to solve the riddle of this astounding amethyst city she must tolerate quite a few things.

In the meantime, Sefner Quorne was a much-baffled man. He was in his space machine, two men to either side of him, and to the rear of his vessel trailed the three companion vessels. He was still trying to fathom a golden fan of light that had abruptly cut off his efforts to destroy the Amazon and Relka. At the moment the golden fan resembled a curtain—a barrier—and it lay a mile distant, blotting out the landscape. Here, where Quorne and his men were flying, there was the normal rocky Saturnian landscape and, some way off, the *Ultra* with its safety lights gleaming.

"I don't understand it," Quorne declared bitterly. "There was no reason why we should not have wiped out the Amazon and Relka completely that time— then came this intervention! Where are they? What's happened to them?"

"Their ship is over there, Excellency," one of the men responded, nodding toward it. "We could destroy it—"

"I'm not interested in that for the moment. It's the Amazon I must find. There is something about this planet I cannot understand. It changes incredibly within seconds. Once before I saw an amethyst city in the wastes and—about here, too!"

"Possibly this golden curtain has something to do with it," one of the men answered.

Quorne turned aside to the analyzing-instrument panel. He spent nearly thirty minutes making tests, during which time the vessel continued a slow circular movement on the outside of the baffling golden curtain which reached to and disappeared in the clouds,

"That curtain is magnetic," Quorne announced. "It is also at an angle to the known three dimensions. It is, in effect, a V-shaped wedge, which has been rotated out of normal space. Technically, it is four-dimensional, but within its area anything of a three-dimensional nature may lie. Altogether, a superb mathematical and scientific achievement," be confessed. "If we decide to penetrate that curtain, two things can happen. We may cross it safely into whatever lies beyond—and doubtless find the Golden Amazon and destroy her; or we might be caught up in the curtain's mysterious composition and be ejected into hyperspace—a non-time area, completely alien, in which we would perish."

# CHAPTER FIVE
## UNSEEN PROTECTOR

The two scientists beside Quorne had no comment to make. They knew him well enough to realize that whatever happened he would follow his own inclinations. It only took him a moment or two to make up his mind.

"We'll risk it," he said, and gave the order to the other machines.

Then he settled at the control board and, his lean face showing the strain he was undergoing at the risk he was taking, he turned the vessel and began to drive it steadily forward. His two companions glanced at one another, then anxiously through the observation port.

The golden curtain swept ever nearer—then the machine struck it. To Quorne's surprise there was no impact, no feeling of electrical reaction. The vessel seemed for a time to travel though whirling golden rain; then passed through it to a vision of a fertile land of intense greenness, its sky blue, its rivers serene. In the distance lay the beauteous amethyst city.

"I was right," Quorne muttered, gazing at it. "That is the same city I saw before—and that, I think, is where we will find the Amazon and Relka."

"What do you propose doing, Excellency?" one of the men inquired. "Blasting the city to make sure of destroying the Amazon?"

"No: that city is too interesting to destroy. Besides, I must make sure first that the Amazon is there. We'll descend and see what we can discover."

Ten minutes later, Quorne walked into the enticing-looking central building just at the moment when the Amazon was at an end of her meal. She and Relka got to their feet as Quorne and his followers entered, their guns ready. The Amazon flashed a glance toward Crinz, but to her amazement he had disappeared.

"We meet in the strangest places, Amazon," Quorne commented, pausing when he had reached the table. "I might even say the most beautiful places. Whoever is the master of this city deserves to be complimented."

There was a sound like masculine laughter, echoing in ghostly waves through the walls and fading into silence. In astonishment Quorne looked about him.

"What was that?" he asked.

"I have not the slightest idea, but I am convinced it is the laughter of the superscientist who rules this city—and who has shown me every hospitality. If you start anything, Quorne, I think you will have to accept all responsibility for what my unseen host may do to you."

Quorne hesitated, then after a moment he gave his acid smile. He placed his gun back in its holster and motioned his men to fall some distance behind him. Coming forward again, he paused within a couple of feet of the Amazon.

"By some unexplained riddle, Miss Brant, you have returned to the field of activity when I thought I had disposed of you. Would I be asking too much if I asked you to explain what happened to you on Ganymede?"

"You would. I don't intend to gratify you."

Quorne shrugged. "Anyway, I think you will agree that the time has arrived when we should decide the issue between us once for all. Both of us seem adept at escaping the fates we plan for each other, so I have a suggestion to make. Since the system cannot hold both of us, let us decide who shall rule—you, or I."

"As far as I am concerned, Quorne, that is not a problem. I shall rule, and I'll spare no energy to hound you out of the system altogether before I'm finished. You wish to bend everything to your will. I am merely anxious to see science progress."

"Very laudable—but at the moment a test of our twin claims to power is the only answer. I have men behind me ready to shoot you down."

The Amazon looked at him steadily her violet eyes aflame.

"What sort of a proposition have you?" she snapped.

"We both have considerable claims to mental power: let us see which is the stronger. Not hypnosis, as that would be a stalemate, I expect." Quorne looked about him then went over to a massive golden ball ornament on a nearby table. He motioned the Amazon to join him.

"Well?" she asked, when she had done so.

Quorne indicated the ball. "We will sit on either side of this table and endeavour to raise this ball into the air by mental power. Or, better still, you will endeavour to raise it. When you have done so, I will exert my will to make it return to the table. If I lose, I will leave the system and never return. If you lose, you will do likewise. Your *Ultra* is still where you left it beyond the golden curtain that surrounds this strange valley, so there is nothing to stop you leaving. That is a pact we must make, and adhere to, as scientists."

The Amazon considered for a moment or two. Her eyes strayed to the distant Jovians on guard, then an idea took hold of her. She gave a nod.

"Very well, Quorne. As you say."

She seated herself at the table, Quorne at the opposite side, the golden ball on its stand between them. For a moment or two they both sat clearing their minds of all outside influences and personal hatreds, then they turned their concentration on the gleaming sphere. The Amazon doubted if she ever could control matter far enough to make it defy the law of the gravity, but she tried hard nevertheless.

She was surprised when the ball quivered slightly, after she had been fixedly studying it for some two minutes. Her hands clenched on the table; her face became rigid. Then, very slowly, the ball began to rise. There was an inch of clearance between it and the tabletop. It hovered, despite its weight of nearly 112 pounds. It began to rise higher, the Amazon raising her eyes to keep them upon it. Then she began to put into practice the idea she had conceived.

As the ball was answering her will, there was no reason why it should not continue to do so. The one thing that puzzled her was the serio-comic nature of the idea she had in mind—it was so unlike her to think of anything humorous.

Quorne watched the ascent of the ball with interest, a thin, half-grudging smile on his lips. Relka watched, too, ready for any action that might be called for. The Amazon still concentrated, and the ball moved forward, hovering now three feet over Quorne's head. Then, suddenly, she released her will power.

Down came the massive globe with terrific impact, striking Quorne on the head with such violence he was flung from his chair, completely stunned, blood oozing from a deep gash across his scalp. There came the sound of hilarious laughter through the great spaces of the building. But the Amazon had no time to listen to it. She overturned the table, whipped out her gun, then hurtled across the room to where Quorne's colleagues had their guns cocked.

At the last second she flung herself down and skimmed along the polished floor. The rays missed her and her hurtling body swept into the men like a ball in a bowling alley. Their feet whipped from beneath them they bowled over helplessly, and two of them never rose as the Amazon's ray-gun slashed murderously across their necks.

The remaining four gained their feet. Two of them found they were grappling with the titanic strength of

Relka. One man in each scaly paw, he whirled them about in blind savagery. The Amazon swung to the remaining two, firing her gun. But the diamond flash-point jammed at the identical moment. She flung the gun away from her and lashed up a terrific left uppercut instead. The nearer man took it under the chin and staggered back a pace. A straight right smashed his nose and sent him whirling against the distant wall.

The two men seized by Relka were hurled in the same direction, dead, their necks at an angle. The remaining man made a dive for the door. Instantly the Amazon leaped after him. One of her hands seized his shoulder; then her right fist came up and down again, crashing with overwhelming force on the root of his skull. He groaned, subsiding into darkness as his vertebrae snapped.

"Which seems to take care of that," the Amazon said, breathing hard and looking about her. "That leaves only Quorne—and the sooner we're rid of him, the better."

She turned and moved toward one of the guns that the guards had dropped, then she hesitated as Quorne, conscious again, seized a gun only a foot away from him. He twisted over, preparatory to firing.

"Out!" the Amazon said abruptly to Relka. "It's our only chance—we're unarmed."

She flung herself toward the doorway, Relka behind her. Just as the Jovian shot beyond the doorway, vicious flame carved a smoking slash in the metalwork. Then, unharmed as yet, the Amazon and Relka were fleeing down the corridor outside.

"Only thing for it," the Amazon panted as she ran. "I thought Quorne was more knocked out than that. I've no spare weapon with me—"

She paused, utterly bewildered. Something inexplicable had happened. She and Relka were no longer racing down a corridor to escape Quorne: they were speeding across rock in the midst of whirling light green vapour toward the lights from a space machine's windows. The wonderland, the city, the oxygen atmosphere—all had gone. The Amazon halted, astounded to discover that she was inhaling ammoniated hydrogen without ill effect. Relka looked at her in the twilight glimmering.

"We're on the plain again," came his thoughts. "But you are not poisoned, Amazon! You're breathing normally."

"I know—and don't ask me why. This planet is unlike anything I ever experienced before.... That's the *Ultra* just ahead," the Amazon finished, as the outlines of the vessel became clear.

She increased her pace, reaching the machine in a few more minutes. Relka followed her through the airlock, then when he had closed the door and the normal air pressure had been restored, he looked at the Amazon inquiringly. In all the time he had known her he had never seen such a look of profound wonderment on her amber-tinted features.

"It defies all natural reasoning!" she declared at last, settling in the control seat and gazing pensively before her. "I am convinced some incredible fourth dimensional manifestation also has a good deal to do with it. And the laughter. It sounded like—Abna."

Relka was silent.

"Perhaps it was," the Amazon mused. "Separated from me by a gulf of time and space. I don't know. Perhaps I never shall. Saturn is a planet that I shall certainly not try to colonize. It is too steeped in mystery. However, I have the present to consider. For the moment, Quorne is out of the running. Perhaps he'll never return from—from wherever we were. In any event, I am going to Jupiter to destroy everything he possesses, and make sure he never again has the power to wage destruction."

She turned to the switches and snapped them in position. With a low humming the power plant began to operate and the vast machine lifted into the green cloud wreathes. And as she drove through the whirling scum the Amazon still found an array of unanswered problems before her. How had she breathed ammoniated hydrogen without harm? Why had she had been impelled to come to Saturn? What serio-comic quirk had led her to drop the gold ball on Quorne's head? And the laughter?

Then she ceased trying to solve the problems, as she had to concentrate on guiding the *Ultra* through the screaming ammoniated hurricanes of the upper levels. At length the vessel burst free of them and into the black quietness of the void, and the Amazon intently studied the detector instruments which she had trained on Jupiter—chiefly to be sure of her course, but some of them were registering other things as well.

"Relka," she called, "what do you make of these?"

He moved from studying the astro-chart screen and joined her. Then he frowned as he surveyed the quivering needles.

"From the look of things, two electromagnetic beams are trained permanently on Earth and Mars," he said. "What it means I don't know, but if Quorne's science is at the back of it, it certainly won't be anything pleasant."

"We have to hurry," the Amazon decided. "We're ahead of Quorne, and he may never reappear from that mystery dimension on Saturn. I shall not rest until his entire city under its protective dome is smashed into ruins, and those who still remain in it are wiped out."

She reached out and the speed lever moved up, notch by notch, in her yellow hand.

\* \* \* \* \* \* \*

Chris Wilson, executive chief of the Dodd Space Line, sat in the lounge of the enormous Earth-Mars space liner. He was a much-worried man, and looked it. Beside him, in a briefcase, were the latest reports on a mysterious disease that had attacked Earth metals.

It was apparent in buildings, machines, ships, aircraft—in fact, everywhere metal was prevalent. Mars also had reported a similar trouble, so Chris was on his way to exchange notes with the analysts on Mars to see what could be done to overcome the trouble. Chris Wilson was more than just the executive chief of the Dodd Line. He was a member of the World Government, and in the absence of the Golden Amazon, who usually handled such matters, he endeavoured to take her place in so far as his normal, limited scientific knowledge allowed.

He did not suspect Sefner Quorne as being the cause of the corrosion trouble. He assumed—as did most scientists—that it was due to some defect in the metals of the present day and age. A metal perhaps which was unstable and which was changing its nature and mutating into some new substance. Chris fervently wished he knew where to reach the Amazon. The last he had heard of her she had been intending to go to Jupiter.

Chris and the other passengers aboard the liner would have been even more alarmed had they known that its outer plates were flaking gently as the machine flew through the void. It was in the very midst of the stream of projectiles being hurled by electromagnetic energy from Jupiter to Mars—Mars being Chris' first destination.

So small were the projectiles in comparison with the mighty liner they were never even noticed by the crew, or if they were, they were assumed to be the normal flying brickbats always encountered in the void.

It was only for a brief period that the liner intercepted the stream of projectiles to Mars—the period when the liner came across the direct line between Jupiter and Mars—but in even that time the damage was done. The nitrine fluid was at work, kept from freezing by the radiation of heat from within the vessel itself, and the solar radiation.

Corrosion was definitely at work, and the liner's engineers were unaware of it—at the moment.

Chris sat back in his seat and mused. Then he snapped out of his reverie as he heard a young woman's voice alongside him: "You don't mind, Mr. Wilson?"

Chris gave a start and looked at the newcomer as she settled herself in the seat next to his. She was strikingly good-looking, with queer coppery-bronze hair and skin that contrasted sharply against the ivory-white two-piece and blouse she was wearing. She had eyes like sapphires.

"You know me?" Chris Wilson asked, surprised.

"You are well known," the girl answered. "I have often wanted to talk to you—if you'll forgive the liberty. My name is Viona. I'm a space traveller. Usually I have my own little flyer, but this time I decided to leave it on Earth and take a liner instead. I like to hear what people talk about, listen to how they think."

"How they think?" Chris looked surprised. "You are a student of telepathy, then?"

"Not just a student, Mr. Wilson. One can acquire many gifts when wandering through the cosmos."

"Yes—I suppose so." Chris looked at her intently.

"I met her on my way to Earth," Viona said.

"Met whom? I didn't mention anyone."

"No, but you thought a good deal. Chiefly about the Golden Amazon. You're anxious to find her because of this corrosion trouble."

"That's right." Chris gave a moody smile. "I can see I shall have to be careful of my thoughts."

Viona laughed. "Have no fear, Mr. Wilson. I'm not the sort of girl to embarrass anybody by exchanging their thoughts with others as common property. I respect the privacy of the individual. You were thinking about the Amazon. She was on Ganymede when I saw her. I was able to render her a small service."

"If only I could contact her," Chris muttered. "She is the only person alive who can deal with this corrosion problem. Do you suppose you might be able to locate her?"

"I might, if I were going in the direction of Jupiter. But I'm not. I'm intending to stay at the Emerson Hotel on Mars for a few months while I study the planet. I find it most absorbing to examine the achievements of the Golden Amazon. She has done so much for the system."

"More than any woman before her," Chris agreed. "If you can call her a woman."

"I can," Viona retorted. "And I do! Because she happens to be stronger and more intelligent than the rest of her sex is no reason to think of her as a—a freak. And that is what you are doing.... I can read it in your mind."

"I speak as I find, Miss Viona," Chris responded. "I have been beside the Amazon for many years—and I long since stopped thinking of her as a woman. She is a machine, pitiless, brilliant, superhumanly strong."

Viona said: "The Golden Amazon has laid the scientific foundations of present-day civilization—but that is only the beginning. Something has already happened which revolutionizes the very law of life itself."

"Forgive me," Chris said politely, "but what are you talking about?"

Viona hesitated, but before she could answer there was a sudden sharp splintering crack like the report of a gun. It came from the curved wall of the lounge. Instantly the other men and women in the expanse looked up quickly. Some got on their feet in alarm. The cracking sound came again and for a moment there was the amazing vision of the opposite wall corroding into dust. Beyond it was the utter emptiness of space with its eternal painting of glowing stars and far distant nebulae.

Instantly air sucked out of the lounge and into space, flinging with it men and women, furniture, and every movable object. Chris too found himself suddenly without the power to breathe. He choked and realized he was being impelled toward that opening through which air was being swept into the vacuum. But he did not reach it. A hand closed on his coat collar and dragged him back. The same hand forced him to turn over so that he lay flat on his face. He was in no condition at that moment to ask questions, or even conjecture. Air was dead: the frightful razor barbs of space were biting into him as the last trace of warmth went from the shattered lounge.

After seconds that seemed eternities he found something being plugged into his mouth. He sucked help-lessly at it and air surged into his lungs again. The same hand seized his shoulder, the other his arm. He was lifted to his feet with an ease that surprised him. His surprise was even greater when he saw it was the slim Viona who was aiding him. She too had one of the emergency air tubes in her mouth—a precaution for passengers, against just such a happening as this. Freezing was not an immediate danger, since a warm body retains its heat by the insulation of the vacuum itself. The air supply was the main thing—and in this case provided by two portable tanks, both of which Viona had slung on to her shoulders.

She jerked her head in a signal and Chris, aided by her surprisingly strong hands, picked his way through the ruined lounge and into the main corridor. Here there was confusion in excelsis. Men and women with air tubes to their faces were striving to reach the small safety machines. Some were succeeding; others were panicked by the thought of being lost in the total void.

Viona looked about her, then at a side corridor. There were five safety ships lined up there, guarded by two of the ship's crew. She hurried forward, Chris beside her, and they immediately barred the way. Instead of allowing them to turn her back, Viona kept going and, releasing Chris for a moment, she seized the nearer officer round the waist and flung him over her head as though he were a rag doll. He landed a dozen feet away, dazed. The second man whipped out his gun. It was snatched from him immediately and a blow across the back of his neck sent him hurtling to crash into his comrade. Viona looked back at them, jerked her head, and in utter bewilderment, Chris followed her to the nearest of the line of safety machines.

She clambered quickly through the open airlock, helped him in after her, then closed the operculum and sealed it. Moving lithely to the control board, she snapped on the power plant. Instantly the vessel detached itself from the gravity plates of the mother ship and sailed out into the void through the ejector chute. In a matter of seconds the corroding liner was a couple of miles away.

Chris removed the air nozzle from his mouth and slipped the canister from where Viona had put it on his shoulder. He moved to where she sat at the control board. Gently he took away her own canister, and her teeth released the nozzle she was unconsciously holding.

"I owe you my life, Miss Viona," Chris said.

She glanced up and smiled brightly. "You are an important man, Mr. Wilson—too important to be whirled away into space to die. I suppose I could have overcome our breathing difficulty by mind force, but I was not prepared for it. I'm not yet completely experienced in mind-over-matter control: takes me some time to sort of—get in the mood."

"That a girl of your age should even think of such an incredible art is beyond me!" Chris confessed. "You can't be much more than twenty, surely?"

"I suppose I do look about that."

This ambiguous answer left Chris more in the dark than before. For a while he studied the view through the windows, then it occurred to him that Mars was not ahead, but Earth.

"You are returning home, then?" he questioned.

"I'm returning you to Earth, Mr. Wilson, and I am also going to get my own space machine and set out to find the Golden Amazon. I hadn't realized how serious this corrosion business had become. You are needed on Earth to keep control of things if they get out of hand. You won't learn anything on Mars except what you already know—and that is that metal everywhere is breaking up."

"Naturally, you read my intended mission from my mind?"

"Some time ago, yes."

"I'm in your hands, Miss Viona," Chris said. "You are about the only person who can locate the Amazon."

"I'd much prefer you dropped the prefix of 'Miss'," Viona said. "Viona is my first, last, and only name."

"Unusual," Chris mused. "Most Earth people have two or more names."

"I am not an Earth woman," Viona explained quite casually.

# CHAPTER SIX
## QUORNE'S DEATH PLAN

Chris' survey of her sharpened. He leaned an elbow on the control bench and watched her as she handled the switches.

She did not look at him. The full glare of spatial sunlight etched out her beautiful young face in finest detail, seemed to accentuate the definitely humorous curves about her mouth and chin. She conveyed the impression that she was enjoying life immensely while still trying to take it seriously.

"If you are not an Earth woman, then who are you?" Chris asked. "The way you saved me, and removed those two men out of the way so we could get a space ship, was almost an exact replica of the Golden Amazon's methods. You even seem to have a similar superhuman strength."

"Perhaps because I admire her so much, I have become like her." Viona laughed, but just the same there was a merry twinkle in her sapphire eyes, which suggested she was holding something back.

"Perhaps," Chris said, unconvinced. "If she had a daughter, I'd imagine her to be exactly like you. A similar type of skin, extraordinary eyes, tremendous energy and strength, and yet with an individuality all your own. You have something the Amazon has not, and never will have."

"I know," Viona assented. "I have a sense of humour. That may be because it takes two of opposite sexes to create one, and the one usually inherits traits from both sides."

Chris gave a start. "Just a moment, my dear! You make it sound as though you are the Amazon's daughter!"

"That's right," Viona said cheerfully. "Only she is not aware of it."

"This is ridiculous!" Chris declared. "You couldn't be the daughter of the Amazon without she herself knowing it!"

"I told you a little while ago that the Amazon had started something which will revolutionize the very laws of life. So I repeat—I am her daughter, but she is not aware of it. Yet."

"You spoke of both sides." Chris was having a tough time keeping a grip on fundamental laws. "Who, then, is your father?"

"Abna of Jupiter. Doesn't my very name suggest that? Viona is an abbreviation of Violet, my mother's name, and the last half of Abna, my father's name. The result is Viona—and me." And she laughed merrily at the blank stare Chris gave her. "It's the truth, believe me. I don't see any reason why you shouldn't know, even though I received instructions not to tell anybody, and my mother least of all. You'll have to know one day, so you might as well now."

"But Abna is dead! What sort of story are you trying to tell me? Abna is dead and your mother—that is, the Amazon—hasn't seen him since he died."

"Perhaps you'd better give it up for the time being," Viona suggested. "It is a bit complicated because it never happened before—but scientifically it is quite logical. And my mother and father deal only in science, not human issues. Neither of them is human, in the accepted sense. They have transcendental powers— and I am the product. And I like it!"

Chris took hold of her slim shoulders, his eyes looking into hers. It was a long, steady look, and the girl gazed at him unflinchingly.

"I'm real enough," she said. "I'm full of fun and crazy ideas, like any young person should be. The trouble with me is I've got too much knowledge and not enough sense. I've been turned loose on the cosmos with tremendous inherited gifts, and I am a bit scared when it comes to using them. I can make matter obey my will and then I wonder if I should. I know most of science from beginning to end. In the normal way, I don't know what fear is, because that is an inherited emotion and is chiefly caused by being born of another human being. Only I wasn't, you see. I just happened."

Chris said: "Even if I never find out how you came into the scheme of things, I like you as I never liked a girl before. You are the Amazon over again, yes, as I said—but in your eyes I can also see the laughter of

Abna. He was a man I intensely respected. In fact, he had only one failing—he would not take anything seriously. I see it being repeated in you."

"When you have the mastery of almost everything, why be serious?" Viona questioned, shrugging. "I suppose that would annoy mother, though."

"It would—and it did. She and Abna—" Chris stopped and sighed. "I don't know what I'm talking about," he finished helplessly.

"You'll understand in time," Viona promised, turning her attention back to the fast-approaching Earth. "If I can get mother to return to Earth, I'll have her tell you everything."

"Suppose your space machine has been destroyed by this corrosion which is affecting everything?"

"I don't think it will be," Viona smiled. "It is different from ordinary space ships. I'm sure it will be all right...."

\* \* \* \* \* \* \*

In silence, her yellow hands on the control switches, the Amazon contemplated the mighty disc of Jupiter as the *Ultra* swept towards it. The machine was invisible to any eyes watching from Jupiter, and upon this she was pinning her hopes.

If she was detected, she was prepared to fight. In any event, her whole being was concentrated on the objective of destroying everything Quorne stood for, and all those who were slaves to his overriding scientific ambitions.

"What is your plan, Amazon?" Relka asked. "Do you propose raining destruction on the domed city from above?"

"That is my intention, yes," the Amazon said. "We will disrupt the dome and allow the poisonous atmosphere to sweep in and kill what Jovians there are in the city; then we will systematically destroy everything. There never was a better opportunity, with Quorne out of the way."

Watching the instruments and x-ray screens for guidance, she plunged the *Ultra* into the whirling cloud belts of the giant planet. Wrapped in this sea-green fog, the vessel hurtled onward and down, until the denser atmospheric layer was penetrated and Jupiter's low, rocky landscape came into view, illumined by the dull twilight which passed for day.

"My calculations are pretty accurate," the Amazon said, glancing up as Relka watched intently. "There is the city dome about ten miles away. Stand by the weapon range. When I fly over the dome release, some of those super-H bombs. They ought to make a fracture in the dome, which is all we need to commence with."

Relka obeyed. Regardless of possible retaliation, the Amazon kept the *Ultra* speeding forward, but at greatly reduced speed. In a matter of minutes she had come close to the gigantic gleaming hemisphere under which the city of the scientists lay protected from the deadly atmosphere. Relka closed his scaly hands over the bomb-release switches.

Then something happened. From a point near the

dome, probably a concealed weapon range, a black segment of non-energy cut across the twilight. Though the *Ultra* was invisible to the eye—if not to instruments—the black ray struck unerringly.

The Amazon stood no chance. The impact of that rotating midnight beam was so terrific that the *Ultra* swung around twice in a wild circle, flinging the Amazon out of her seat and against the wall. She struck it with her head and the universe burst into fiery stars. She tried to get to her feet, but the *Ultra* was spiralling and turning over and over. She and Relka both turned somersaults. Now they were on the floor, now the walls, now the ceiling. Flung around like a leaf in the fall gale, the *Ultra* descended to the rock plain—and struck it with blinding force. Even the shock-absorbing springs did not save it this time.

The Amazon felt as if a hammer had struck her on top of the head. Everything cascaded into flaming stars and she dropped stunned to the floor.

\* \* \* \* \* \* \*

When her senses began drifting back to her, she realized that she was lying amidst bright lights. She was on her back, passably comfortable, an air cushion supporting her head. She opened her eyes wider and studied the face looking down on her. It was thin, intensely cynical, and intelligent, with eyes the colour of heliotrope.

"Better, Miss Brant?" Sefner Quorne asked pleasantly.

In sudden fury, the Amazon grasped the situation. She sat up and got to her feet, her hand flying to her gun belt. But she had had no weapon in it—she did not even have the belt. It had been removed. Her eyes flashed from Quorne to Relka, standing bound with a tough chain nearby. Beyond him were the scientists of this master city—this one-time Atlantis.

"You seem to be meeting with quite a few misfortunes, Miss Brant," Quorne commented. "Perhaps you are commencing to lose your touch. You should not have been so reckless as to think that you could destroy this city by a direct approach. Instruments kept a constant watch on you."

"And obviously you escaped Saturn?" the Amazon snapped at him.

"Obviously. It was not easy. I chased after you, only to find myself on the former plain with the non-existent amethyst city. I succeeded in containing my breath long enough in the poison atmosphere to reach one of my four machines, and so I escaped and returned here, to learn what you had intended to do. I will grant you one last favour before I destroy you. You know that I have electromagnetic beams trained on Earth and Mars. They are carrying destruction to those worlds in the form of rust. Before very long every scrap of metal on those worlds will crumble.... Now, I have told you that, I have no other task to perform except destroying the pair of you."

The Amazon did not answer, but her violet eyes glared defiance.

Quorne turned to the disintegrator and adjusted the nozzle. When it was to his liking, he lowered his hand to the firing switch—then with a sudden vicious movement closed it.

Brilliant lavender tight enveloped the Amazon and Relka close beside her. Both of them disappeared in a blinding flash. The scientists in the laboratory blinked for a moment and saw nothing but dispersing smoke and in the midst of it Quorne's icily satisfied features.

* * * * * * *

Ten thousand miles from Jupiter a lone space machine was slowing down after travelling from Earth at nearly the speed of light. At the controls Viona sat alone. Originally she had set off to try to find the Golden Amazon, but the streak of adventure and daring was strongly ingrained within her, and by this time she had come to the conclusion that perhaps she could handle the matter herself.

Interception of two of the hurtling projectiles had shown her that they contained a fluid that could destroy metal: the rest was mere deduction. They were being hurled from Jove, so the thing to do was track down their exact source on Jove and stop them. Even the Amazon herself could not do more than that.

The problem confronting Viona was how to land on Jove without attracting suspicion; then she hit on the simplest method of all. She had only to come down with a broken rocket tube and pretend to be a space traveller in distress, then work things out from that basis. Since she was quite an unknown quantity as yet—unlike the Amazon—she saw no reason why her strategy would not work.

So she began lowering her machine to the mighty planet, and as she did so she allowed the power in one of the forward rockets to increase itself beyond the danger point. The result was inevitable. The tube fractured with the terrific heat. It demanded considerable skill on her part to lower the machine through the screaming ammonia tempests—but gradually she accomplished it, keeping a close watch on the screens.

She landed the machine cleverly. Then she switched off the lights to give the impression that the impact had caused a short circuit. She knelt before the tilting observation window and gazed out of the twilight gloom embracing the plain, waiting for something to happen.

She had no real guarantee that anything would, and if not, she was prepared to commence an exploration. But she could not imagine the scientists of Jove operating their deadly beams upon the inner planets allowing a space ship to land without inquiring into it.

And she presently caught a glimpse of searchlights sweeping the rocky terrain as investigating machines came speeding through the tumultuous heavens. She waited until they were close, then she threw herself face down in a corner and simulated unconsciousness.

Before long she heard the sizzling of metal as the airlock was pried open, followed by a singing as air whistled out of her machine. She was wondering whether or not to go on breathing by mind control when she found herself lifted in powerful hands and a space suit was dragged over her. Its air cylinder began to function. She was raised again, and watching through her eyelashes, a performance that was masked by her helmet visor, she saw herself carried into one of the rescue machines. Here she was laid down on a wall bunk. She kept her eyes shut.

A needle jabbing into her arm made her wince, so she opened her eyes and looked about her. Intelligent but unsmiling faces were looking down on her, all the faces of men. Some of them were in white and wearing rubber gloves. Others were in tight purple robes. Around and behind them loomed the equipment of a surgery.

Viona said nothing for a moment. Her brain was busy reading the minds of the beings about her, and she did not particularly like what she detected. Then, certain of which man was Sefner Quorne, she looked directly at him.

"I trust you are commencing to recover from your accident, traveller?" he asked, in his most courteous voice.

Viona sat up on the air-cushioned table on which she had been lying. She nodded and smiled.

"Thank you, yes. Fortunate, too, that you understand English." Viona looked deliberately mystified. "But I cannot understand what race you are. I thought Jupiter was uninhabited."

"We are descendants of Atlantis, and therefore at

root are Earth people," Quorne replied. "I hope we can show you every hospitality while you are here. If you will come with me, we can talk and have a meal while I have your space machine repaired. I'm afraid it was badly damaged. You should have known better than try and play tricks with the tremendous gravity of this planet."

"I haven't been an aviatrix very long," Viona explained.

"I see." Quorne's eyes measured her. "For a girl who has not been an aviatrix for long, you have come a considerable distance from the normal space lanes."

"That is simply explained. I have a passion for exploring."

Quorne did not comment. Thought reading was an art he possessed, but he rarely used it—and this time it did not please him very greatly when he discovered the girl's mind was a complete blank. She was either extremely unintelligent, or else such a master of thought that she knew how to defend herself.

"I offer you my hospitality," he said. "My name is Quorne—Sefner Quorne, and I have absolute authority in this city. And your name?"

"Minton." Viona answered, using the first name that came into her head. "Christine Minton, of Earth."

He conducted the girl down the corridors and finally into his private suite, and five minutes later she found herself seated before a resplendent meal.

"The people of Earth are well known to me," he said. "I imagine you will be aware of that fact, since not so very long ago I ruled them."

"By hypnosis, you mean? Yes. I heard about that."

"Heard about it? Were you not present among those who had sworn allegiance to me?"

"No. I have been travelling in space for many years— but I heard when I got back how your regime had been broken up by the Golden Amazon." Viona glanced up for a moment. "Believe me, Excellency Quorne, it is no concern of mine who rules the Earth or anywhere else. I'm just a wanderer of the spaceways, with no fixed abode."

"You are very young to do that. You are also very beautiful. I will go further: you are every whit as beautiful as the woman who defeated me when I ruled Earth."

"You mean the Amazon? You pay me a great compliment, Excellency. There is nobody I would sooner resemble. I have seen the Amazon personally but once—and I have not forgotten it."

"Would that once be on Ganymede?" Quorne inquired politely. He met her brief startled look with a steady eye.

"I feel, Miss Minton, that you are playing a very dangerous game," he said. "I admire you for it. Before you go any further, I think you ought to know that your space ship is the same one which I, and several of my colleagues, saw leaving Ganymede quite some time ago. I don't think you would have come here had you been aware that your vessel was so well known to us."

Viona was young and inexperienced, but she had no

real conception of fear. So she smiled cheerfully.

"I couldn't help myself coming here, Excellency. My ship got an overheated tube and it fractured. I just crashed, and that was that."

"If you came here in the hope of finding the Amazon, Miss Minton, you have had a journey in vain. She is dead. I killed her, and her Jovian companion, only a few hours ago. I make no apology for that. All the system knows that she and I were the deadliest of enemies."

Viona did not speak but her lack of years was commencing to give her away. She tried desperately to stop the glimmer of tears she felt surging to her eyes.

"Very touching," Quorne commented. "You weep on hearing of her death. Perhaps you are—or were—related to her."

Viona still tried to hide her feelings—not very successfully.

"For all I know," Quorne continued, "you may be a synthetic creature she created during her extraordinary career, a creature working under post-hypnotic orders—which orders will undoubtedly be to dispose of me. On the other hand, you could be a relative, though it is queer I have not been aware of it. You have much about you that suggests the late Amazon—I knew little of her private life, of course, so I suppose a daughter is not so impossible."

Viona got to her feet, her young face resolute, her blue eyes gleaming.

"All right, so you have guessed the truth," she said fiercely. "My real name is Viona, and I am the daughter of the Golden Amazon. I'm here on this planet to do what she evidently failed to do—smash you and all your works."

Quorne laughed softly. "With your inexperience and that still immature body? You would be much more sensible to accept my hospitality, Viona, until I shall decide what to do with you."

"I know already what you intend to do with me—I've read your mind. You intend to use me as you tried once to use my mother—to make her the basis of a new race. You failed with her, and you will with me."

Quorne's expression changed. Striding around the table, he gripped one of Viona's arms tightly.

"Very well, since you know my plans, there is no point in my repeating them—but let me add that we of Atlantis are a dying race because only males are left. We are interested in the biological fact that you are a perfect female. Just as your mother was. She proved too clever for us—but you will not. You have not her experience or scientific agility."

Viona's eyes were aflame with anger, not so much against Quorne as against herself for having made such a hopeless mess of her effort to cross swords with the most dangerous scientist in the solar system.

"With you as the basis of a new Atlantean race, we can produce the most perfect men and women," Quorne continued, musing. "The plan we had for your mother can be used with you—" He paused, frowning suddenly. "And who is your father?" he snapped. "What man could there be that the Amazon would deign to marry?"

"My father is Abna, the royal dignitary whom you betrayed."

Quorne released his grip and stared at the girl.

"Abna died," he said at length. "I found his dead body in this very city when I took it over again. That was no more than a year ago. Yet you are at least twenty. Twenty years ago your mother did not even know Abna. You're lying!"

"No. I'm not lying." She shook her head, and the copper-bronze hair caught the concealed lighting. "An unbelievable thing happened. I was born by a process which, if you but knew it, would do away with all this biological business you're thinking up to restart your race."

"I must know that secret," Quorne snapped. "There is no scientific process of which I intend to remain in ignorance. Tell me about it."

His hand reached out again for the girl's arm, but at the same moment she twisted to one side. Swinging back again, she slammed up her right fist under Quorne's jaw. The impact was so great that it sent him sprawling helplessly backward across the table.

# CHAPTER SEVEN
## TRAPPED BY EVIL

Viona felt for her gun, but it had been taken from the belt about her slacks. So she hurtled at Quorne again, just as he was staggering to his feet. Again that superhuman fist, so reminiscent of the Golden Amazon herself, smashed into his face, flattening him. He was left gasping for breath. His gun was gone and his watering eyes were fixed on a slim feminine figure racing to the door.

Viona wrenched it open and darted out into the corridor. One of the guards yanked out his gun, and the next he was grappling with a slender form that seemed to be made of uncoiling springs. Wherever he gripped, his hand slid away. Finally he received a vicious crack on the back of the neck that brought him down. Immediately Viona was astride his back, her right arm bent under his jaw.

"Quickly—some information!" she panted. "Where is the laboratory which is sending the magnetic beams to the inner planets?"

The guard fought frantically to free himself, but the armlock under his chin became all the tighter. Slowly his head was being forced at a sharp angle to his verte-brae.

"I don't want to kill you," Viona told him, "but I must have the information, and your mind's too clouded for me to read it. Tell me!"

"B-back down—the corridor—" the guard gasped, half-fainting with pain, and immediately Viona released him and sprang up, to see Quorne emerge, dishevelled and blood-streaked, from his suite. She fired the gun at him and he dodged back.

She ran down the corridor, but a heavy metal door barred the way to the laboratory. It was locked and she swung her gun on it, but there was no time for using it. Quorne, with several guards, all of them armed, was running toward her.

Viona looked about her desperately, fired one blast of her gun to check the onrush, and then dived for the only way of escape—a massive staircase.

She pelted up it, flight after flight, and finally it brought her out on the flat roof of the building. The pursuers were coming nearer. She glanced about her and saw numberless aircraft and space flyers. Quickly she moved to the nearest spaceship and leaped through its airlock and to the control board. Starting up the plant, which seemed to be of the conventional atomic pattern, she swept the vessel upward for perhaps fifty feet, then turned it directly downward.

Its nose struck the open trapdoor just as Quorne and his men were struggling up the final twenty steps. They were blocked completely.

Viona sped to the roof parapet. She knew now where the source of the magnetic beams lay—on the ground level—and the problem was to reach them before Quorne raised a warning. Running to the machine she had upended, she took down the emergency coil of steel rope carried in every machine. With it in her hand she sped back across the roof, leaped the gap to the neighbouring roof, then secured the wire tightly around a parapet projection. The other end of the wire she coiled around her forearms.

She sized up the long drop that was between her and the windows of the ground floor scientific laboratory. Then she jumped, flashed downward in a huge arc, and released herself with split-second timing. Feet first, she crashed through the laboratory's enormous main window, the non-injurious glass crumpling into powder around her.

There were quite a few scientists in the huge place, and they swung around in amazement at her whirlwind arrival. None of them was armed, a fact she quickly noted, probably because this laboratory was assumed to be impregnable.

Her eyes glanced about quickly and centred on a huge power plant occupying the central floor space. She motioned one of the scientists toward her with the gun, and he obeyed her.

"You can save your life by answering one question," she said curtly. "Where is the machinery which is sending electromagnetic beams to Earth and Mars?"

The man set his mouth stubbornly, but since she was

concentrating on his brain she received an immediate clear picture of the information she wanted. The man's greatest fear seemed to be for a filigree of vital wires in the centre of the instrument concerned—and the instrument was the one occupying the centre of the floor.

"Never mind," Viona told him, and raced across to the huge equipment.

She looked at the array of switches, glowing panels, banks of insulators, the whole mass of technical equipment—then she saw the section that had been briefly mirrored in the mind of the man she had questioned. It was obviously the heart of the amazing apparatus— a criss-crossed maze of thousands of numbered wires and chips, which must have taken many months to put into correct position.

The engineers hesitated, not quite sure what she was going to do, and by the time they had started moving it was too late. She raised her gun and sighted it on the 'heart', and the jetting flame severed the entire complicated mass. There was the sound of exploding components, and in the distance an enormous earthing-rod ejected a cloud of electric sparks.

Viona swung, her gun ready, but she was not quick enough to prevent her arms being seized. She was gripped tightly and held, her gun torn from her grip. At the same moment the distant door of the laboratory opened ponderously, and the dishevelled Sefner Quorne came in, followed by his guards.

His face black with fury, he hurried over to where

Viona was pinioned, her back against the machine she had destroyed.

"You fools! Idiots!" he screamed at the engineers. "Are you incapable of stopping a mere girl like this from wrecking the equipment? Look at it! Look at it! The wire matrix is utterly ruined. It will take months to reassemble it."

In outraged temper he swung back to Viona, and slapped her violently across the face both ways.

"We didn't know what she intended doing, Excellency," one of the scientists protested. "Nobody told her anything, yet she somehow knew the one vital part in the equipment to wreck."

"She can read thoughts, you fool—that's the answer," Quorne yelled at him. "I'll make you suffer for this later. Get this girl out of here," he commanded, jerking his head to the guards. "Take her to the surgical laboratory, and when you get her there, chain her down. She has as much strength as the Golden Amazon herself."

Viona fought mightily, but strong though she was, the weight of numbers was against her. Firmly held, she was lifted from her feet and carried away. Quorne swung his attention back to the shattered mechanism.

"Clear away the damage from this equipment and then go to work repairing it," he ordered. "In the meantime, the projectiles to the inner planets are held up."

"Those that have already been sent will have done a good deal of damage, Excellency," one of the men commented.

"I don't doubt it, but that isn't the point. That infernal

girl has upset my arrangements—and I'll make her suffer for it."

He swung away and hurried from the laboratory, arriving in the surgery a few minutes later. Viona was lying on her back on an operating table, her arms fastened to her sides, thick straps over her neck, waist, and ankles. She glared defiantly at Quorne as he came within her line of vision.

"Though it will take me a long time to repair the damage you have caused, I will refrain from killing you in retaliation," he said, measuring his words. "I said earlier that you will be useful as the first female of our race—but you alone are not sufficient. I need hundreds like you, an ideal pattern—for synthetic robots who will duplicate you in every detail. That was the plan I had for your mother; now I can use it for you."

Quorne considered for a while, then added: "You will not enjoy this process of electronic patterning. Every nerve and organ will be probed electrically, the vibrations from those nerves and organs being transmitted to synthetic flesh, just as light waves excite the silver salts of a film and reproduce an exact image of the object photographed. When I have finished, there will be hundreds of synthetic Vionas, who will be the basis for the female side of our race."

Viona squirmed a little in the straps, but she was powerless to free herself. Quorne looked about him on the waiting surgeons.

"Proceed," he ordered, and then stood back to supervise operations.

\* \* \* \* \* \* \*

From out of intense darkness in which nothing lived or moved the Amazon began to emerge. Strange sensations passed through her. The first sensation indeed since that ghastly moment when her entire being had been ripped asunder by the shattering impact of Quorne's disintegrator beam. Now there was a feeling of drowsiness, yet with it an intense tingling, gradually becoming more intense until she found it nearly unbearable. She analyzed it as the circulation of blood through blocked arteries.

With an effort she opened her eyes and it felt like an activity she had never performed before. Immediately she shut them again as light hit her. She tried again, and this time accustomed herself. Overhead was a flawlessly white high ceiling, somehow radiating light within itself. She had only seen such an effect as that once before, and that had been in Millennia, the amethyst city.

Amethyst city? Her heart began to beat more rapidly. She had been on Jupiter when she had been disintegrated: it seemed impossible that she could be on Saturn now, yet—she raised herself on her elbow. Then she frowned. She was not in the black suit she usually wore when in space, but in robes of regal purple. The sweeping gown went down to her feet, and upon her feet were shoes made of material like cloth-of-gold, a strap of diamonds holding them in position.

"Hello, Vi!"

As the melodious voice reached her, the Amazon

turned her head sharply: then she stared in utter incredulity. A giant was nearby, a smiling, blond-headed man who stood seven feet tall, his short tunic enhancing his enormous muscular development and magnificent limbs. He had blue eyes, drily humorous, and the face of a god. Behind him loomed the yellow of golden machinery.

"Abna!" the Amazon whispered, fascinated. "Abna! Is it you? Or am I dreaming?"

"No, you're not dreaming," he assured her in the casual way he had. He came forward and sat on the edge of the long table on which she was half lying. "I thought it was about time I stopped playing games with you and came into the open. When you got yourself killed, I had to do something.... And I did. You are as alive as you ever were."

"But you— I just don't understand! Abna, if this is a mind projection, or something, stop playing jokes with me. I couldn't stand it."

"I don't suppose you could, after the beating you've been taking lately. You haven't accomplished one useful thing against Quorne!"

"Just the way it happened—" The Amazon's eyes glinted suddenly and she sat up straight. "What do you know about my activities?"

"I know all about them, and I have helped you out of one or two sticky positions. I don't expect any thanks because you are incapable of gratitude. I don't forget the way you ditched me on Io."

"And I don't forget how you hurled me way beyond

the solar system in retaliation!"

"I knew you'd get back, otherwise I wouldn't have done it."

The Amazon looked steadily at Abna's half-smiling face. There was upon it the indulgent expression of a man humouring a fractious child, that expression which always infuriated the Amazon beyond measure. She got off the surgical table and stood up beside him, the top of her head reaching to his vast shoulders.

"How little you change, Vi," he commented.

"I might say the same of you," she retorted. "Stop being so condescending."

"I'm not being condescending; that is simply the way in which you interpret it. However, we have much to talk about. Come and have a meal—same room as before."

"As before?" The Amazon glanced up at him in surprise.

"Certainly. You are in Millennia, and I know you enjoyed the last meal I had prepared for you. Remember Crinz?"

"Certainly I remember him. I suppose he was another of your jokes?"

"No—not a joke. A mind projection. A man who never really existed except for the brief time I created him."

The Amazon east a look around on the golden instruments of the surgery, and then walked through the doorway which Abna had indicated, and so into that enormous room already familiar to her. At the table a meal had been laid for two. There was no other person present.

The Amazon kicked impatiently at the entangling folds of the robes she was wearing, then seated herself. Abna settled opposite her.

"For the queen of the system, my dear, your behaviour does not become you," he remarked. "You should be proud to wear the royal robes of Atlantis. In fact, they mean even more than that. You have long been the uncrowned queen of the solar system: now I have raised you officially to that status. You may resent the idea of my being king, and higher in authority than you, but there it is."

The Amazon swallowed her indignation and the hot retort that sprang to her mind. She was burningly eager to know what had happened to bring the genial giant of Jupiter back into her life.

"It is a long story, and a strange one," Abna told her, as he held a golden dish for her to select what she would eat. "A story of the triumph of mind over matter. I will not go into detail because you would not understand it."

"Do you have to be insulting?" she snapped.

"I'm stating a fact, Vi. And you know it! When I died on Jupiter under that falling girder," he continued, "I completely lost control of the situation. I was then a being of flesh and blood who had never died, and for the moment I was afraid—desperately afraid. Then as I sank down into the coma of death, I remembered something. I had once saved Ethel, your foster niece, from death when she had been seriously injured. I once saved you from death, too. Both of those instances were mind over matter. Could I accomplish the same tremendous control for myself? I was sinking at that very moment, poison air swirling about me, my body crushed by the girder. I exerted my powers to the limit. My mind cleared remarkably—indeed, it reached a new level I had never experienced before! I found I could swallow the ammonia gas without harm. That gave me strength again. I dragged myself free of the girder."

The Amazon waited and Abna went on talking, half to himself, half to her.

"I suppose," he mused, "I was actually dead physically, but my mind still lived on—and on a new transcendental level. The mind is indestructible, and I have proved it. Anyway, from that moment on, so complete was my mastery of myself, I was able to do many things mentally which I had not done before. I decided to continue a few experiments in mind force—but not on Jupiter. I wanted somewhere quiet, so I selected Saturn. I created this city."

"Single-handed?" the Amazon asked in amazement.

"By mind force," he replied. "I willed it into being. It is not difficult, because matter always obeys mind. However, I had hardly domiciled myself here before Quorne invaded my privacy, and after that you came."

The Amazon nodded, and Abna went on: "I detected both of you by the impact of your minds reacting on mine. At that stage I did not wish either of you to disturb me, so I willed my city out of existence and it vanished. I realized, from the mind-waves I was receiving, that Quorne was intending to domicile himself on Jupiter again, so I thought it as well to let him think I had really died. I went to Jupiter ahead of him by instantaneous mind-transportation. There I left a synthetic double of myself under the girder that had hit me. Then I came back here."

The Amazon nodded slowly. Her resentment had cooled completely before the recital of scientific facts,

"What you really mean is: you have completely mastered the secrets of mind force?"

"I believe so. Some things even yet do not bow to my mental waves, but most do. That means that I can create what I wish, where I wish. I decided to enjoy myself by teaching you a lesson and improving my technique at the same time."

"You—what?"

"Sorry, Vi—but for a long time you have been needing something in return for the way you treated me. Remember? I married you in good faith because I loved you and respected you—and what did you do? You replaced the real archbishop with a synthetic image, told me the marriage was not legal, and then ditched me. You just couldn't bear the thought of my being stronger than you, could you?"

"In my own way I am still the mistress of all scientific developments," she retorted, "I am not beholden to any man, and don't intend to be."

"Scientist versus woman," Abna chuckled. "Never

stop being a scientist, do you? Except for the brief time when you really did think we could make a life of scientific achievement together. However, to come back to the point. I decided you should have me mentally. By careful mental searching, I succeeded in contacting your mind, and thereafter I constantly held you in thought. I compelled you to see me, and this city of mine. I forced you for long spells to be with me in mind, if not in body—and you succumbed completely."

"Hypnosis," the Amazon muttered. "Now I understand. I sensed all the time I was with you, but could not understand it."

"Now you know. I always kept a protective watch on you. You wanted to defeat Quorne and so establish your supremacy in the solar system. Twice I deflected you from going to Jupiter when I knew it would mean certain death. I forced you to come here instead. I was mentally watching your every move, and when I saw Quorne seemed likely to destroy you, I willed my city into being and shut him out. He explained the mystery to himself as being four-dimensional. A mental creation never occurred to him. In this city, when you wandered through it," Abna continued, "I revealed all the things I knew would appeal to you. Precious stones, power-houses of gold, all the things a man likes to give to the woman he loves. You were suitably impressed, but baffled. I created a servant for you. I let you think you lifted a golden ball, then I dropped it on Quorne's head and gave you the idea it was your own notion—"

"You what?" the Amazon broke in, startled. "You

mean you did that?"

"Certainly. Didn't you hear me laughing? I was there all the time, but since matter can obey mind, I had made myself invisible. I could have dealt with Quorne myself, but I wanted you to try and master Quorne in your own way. But you failed—and again I had to rescue you. I changed your mental state so you could breathe poison gas, and you escaped in your *Ultra.* Quorne, too, I allowed to escape because I believed you wanted to continue the struggle against him. You did—and got killed."

"And you put me together again?" the Amazon asked, with a sceptical glance.

"I did, yes. But I had to use instruments, as my mind was not strong enough to perform reintegration of thousands of scattered atomic clusters. I had followed you to Jupiter, first by x-ray television, and then mental projection to see how you fared—"

The Amazon frowned. "Mental projection?"

"Yes. Television observation has its drawbacks because it is not instantaneous over interplanetary distances, whereas mind force—when concentrated—can move instantaneously and is not limited to the speed of light. When I realized that Quorne had you at his mercy, and was going to kill you by using that disintegrator on you, I returned here instantly and trained my magnetic instruments and dissembler beam—in that golden powerhouse you have already seen—intending to snatch you back, as I did once before on Earth. Unfortunately this time I was a fraction too late.

Even though I sent the dissembler beam through the fourth dimension, so that it was instantaneous, Quorne had already blasted you. Instead, my dissembler beam reacted upon the spot where your atomic clusters were still floating. You were still there, but disembodied, your body exploded into atomic aggregates. I withdrew them here. After that it was only a matter of reassembly of the atoms in the normal way when an object has been sent a distance. Your mind force was still gravitating amidst those atoms, in a quiescent state— so it came back to its normal function when you had been restored atom for atom, every part of you fitting back into your natural physique. Since I didn't bring your clothes as well, I considered you would be best attired in royal regalia."

There was a long silence when Abna had concluded speaking. By this time the Amazon had finished her meal. She relaxed a little; then a thought struck her.

"And Relka, my Jovian friend?"

"I'm sorry, Vi, but I couldn't restore him. By the time I had dealt with you, his atomic aggregates were too widely scattered."

"Or maybe you didn't want to? You don't want me to rely on anybody except you, do you? Well, that is where you are mistaken in me, Abna. I will not be dominated; I have too much individuality of my own for that."

"I don't wish to dominate you, Vi. I ask only one thing—that we work side by side for the good of the system. You are a brilliant scientist and I have the mastery of matter. What more do we need than that to help the lesser beings to understand and finally master the universe?"

"We need much more—a common bond of understanding. We have not got it. I once thought we had—"

"It's no use, Vi," Abna said quietly. "I can read your mind, remember. You won't admit that you have missed me, that the period when you thought I was dead was misery to you. You are too proud to confess that you can surrender yourself to a man—even such a man as I."

The Amazon got to her feet and stood majestically by the table.

"Conceit again, Abna!" she reminded him.

"Not conceit—just truth. I know I have the powers of a god, but I use them wisely. Conceit does not enter into it." He rose, too, his hands closing gently about her shoulders.

"Listen, Vi. Things are different now than in the earlier days when we first met, when we tried to outdo each other in efficiency. There is another to consider, one who looks to us for an example."

"Whom, for instance?"

"Viona. You have already met her: I saw to it that you did."

"Yes, I have. She—" The Amazon stopped, her eyes widening. She looked up at Abna's smiling face. "She restored me from injury and repaired my *Ultra*. She—she also talked a good deal about mind force."

"I know," Abna laughed. "Children are usually proud of the gifts they inherit from their parents, are they not?"

"Children? Parents? What do you mean? Viona is a young woman of twenty at least...."

"Viona is your daughter, Vi—and mine."

# CHAPTER EIGHT
## ABNA'S SECRET POWER

Never in her life had the Amazon looked so astounded. It made Abna laugh all the more, and his arm tightened about her.

"I thought you'd guess it from her name," he said.

"I did suspect, but then I realized how impossible it must be."

"It is not impossible. It happened. She is the product of your mind and mine. Probably she is the first living being to be created by a union of thought. She was born at the age she is now, and like you and me—who have life which is measured only in hundreds of years—she will remain that apparent age for centuries to come. She is the first of the mental children of a superman and superwoman. We have found a new law of life, Vi."

"You mean you have!" the Amazon declared, bewildered. "I didn't know anything about it."

"Not consciously, perhaps. It happened when you and I were in a union of thought, which you mistook for hypnosis. Remember how often we were together? With my newly enhanced mastery over matter, I envisaged the kind of child I would like to have. I fashioned thought forms in the air as a sculptor moulds clay. I did not like the creations I made; then your impressions became mixed with mine, and there followed a dual effort of mental creation. I performed the concentration while your own thoughts fused with mine. Out of nothing, formed directly by mind force on empty space—which is full of matter but invisible—there emerged an image. It became Viona, fully grown, gifted with my knowledge and yours—yet having her own personality as every living thing has. It was a gentle, delicate thing, this birth, Vi, as sweet as a dream, as absolute as life itself."

To this the Amazon had nothing to say. She sat down again and gazed in front of her, her mind going back to a time when, in apparent hypnosis, she had collapsed on the floor of her laboratory and had experienced an amazingly vivid dream with Abna as the central figure, Now she remembered—and understood.

"This changes everything, Abna," the Amazon whispered, her tone entirely unresentful. "You have accomplished the ideal of all lesser mortals—created, without hurt and material intervention. There were facets in Viona's character which made me wonder...."

"Viona is the guarantee that the breach between us must be closed," Abna said decisively. "You are mine, and I am yours. Between us we have a Universe to put to rights. To destroy all the little, evil things, to bring to ruin and destruction such power-lusters as Quorne and those who follow him."

"Agreed," the Amazon responded quietly. "I can fight the issue no more, Abna; after this revelation I would not wish to. But where is Viona now? I haven't seen her since she appeared on Ganymede."

"Whither I dispatched her to save you. I told her to keep quiet about her identity, since I wanted to see if you could find out the truth for yourself."

"The sooner she is found, the better— Which reminds me," the Amazon broke off. "I had forgotten the mission I was on when I was wiped out by Quorne. He is destroying the cities of the inner planets by some rusting process. That has to be stopped—and Viona located."

"The laboratory can tell us all we need to know."

They went into a bewildering place wherein instruments of solid gold caught the reflective light.

Abna moved to a complicated radio-telescopic device and sat down in the control chair. Under his hand the lights supplied so mysteriously by the walls died out and intense dark descended. Then a giant screen came into life, sunken into the floor, and upon it was mirrored a picture of Sefner Quorne's major laboratory on far-away Jupiter. A group of Atlantean scientists were at work on a massive wiring mesh, and to judge from their expressions they were not enjoying their task.

"They seem to be making a repair of some kind," the Amazon said.

"Apparently."

"Try your detectors, Abna, and see if there are any

electromagnetic beams projecting from Jupiter toward the inner planets."

Abna turned to his instruments and studied the readings in the glow of the spotlight.

"Nothing there," he said. "Space is free."

"Which means that somehow the apparatus causing those electromagnetic beams has been put out of action," the Amazon said, her eyes gleaming. "And from the look of things, that shattered wire mesh has something to do with it. From that it seems logical to think that only Viona could have caused such a disaster to Quorne."

"Viona must be on Jupiter then," Abna said.

He set to work with the telescopic controls and the scene on the screen began to change. Oblivious to walls and barriers, the probing x-ray beam passed through the buried city, and as it crossed a surgery it stopped.

"There she is!" the Amazon cried. "And Quorne!"

In silent horror Abna watched the gathering of surgeons around the slender figure buckled to an operating table. Near the struggling Viona was a bath of stainless metal, in which reposed a pile of a substance resembling putty. To the bath electrodes were connected, their trailing wires leading back to suction cups that the surgeon was now fixing to various parts of Viona's body.

"Synthesis!" the Amazon snapped. "Quorne is using Viona as a master pattern—as he once tried to do it with me. We can't possibly get to Jupiter in time to—"

Abna switched off the apparatus and got to his feet

quickly.

"There's one way to do it," he said, "and that is by mental transportation. Only...no, I'm forgetting, you are not intelligent enough."

The Amazon flared at him: "What you can do, I can do, and—"

"No, you can't, Vi. We'll have to use material means. Atomic transference."

"Of course! The same method you used to snatch me from Earth and Jupiter." She shot Abna an anxious look as he stood hesitating. "Then what are you waiting for? Do it now—"

"No, Vi," Abna cut her short. "Snatching Viona directly just cannot be done so quickly. The calculations needed are immense and will take time. When I transported you, I had been forewarned, and the calculations already worked out."

"Then what—?"

Abna began moving decisively. "I can set the machine more or less immediately to transmit us to Jupiter, just outside the dome." He handed her a spacesuit. "Get into this, quickly. I don't really need one, but I'll put it on and save myself a lot of mental effort defeating Jove's poison atmosphere."

The Amazon took the spacesuit handed to her and scrambled into it. In a matter of seconds she and Abna were screwing on the helmets. Then after an inspection to be sure their weapons were in order, Abna led the way to the transmission plates of his spatial projector. "My machine incorporates the fourth dimension, so our transit to Jupiter will be instantaneous," he explained. He set the master controls, switched on the power, then held the Amazon close beside him as, gradually, the uncanny power of the instrument began to function.

Even though the Amazon was accustomed to the transmission of her atomic components through space, it still did not make the feat any the less startling. There was that brief period of dizziness and intense dark and the plucking of nerve fibres by electronic currents. Then a sense of headlong falling, a roaring in her ears, and gradually the deadening mist of the transition cleared from before her eyes.

Beside her was Abna in his spacesuit. Ahead was the gleaming hemisphere that was the dome over the Atlantean city.

"We're going to be too late," the Amazon said, switching on her audio-phone. "By this time the operation will have started."

"Maybe, but Viona cannot come to any real harm by just being a pattern, even though she may endure a good deal of discomfort. Not that she need even endure that if she remembers to make her body immune to pain by mind force.... Anyway, we have to get inside the dome. Come."

The Amazon did not ask how the feat was to be accomplished. They reached the mighty hemisphere, and looked at the city far below.

"Smashing this dome would let in the poison air and kill them all," the Amazon said. "Just as it did on a past occasion."

Abna said: "True—but Viona, too, would die if she didn't remember in time to master her body against the poison, or she might not if she is dazed by the operation she is undergoing. We'll have to pass through the dome. I came prepared for that."

"By mind force, you mean?"

"No. You couldn't do that and I doubt if I could do it for both of us. No—with this."

From his instrument belt Abna took an object like a flashlight and began adjusting its focus.

"Just an improvement on one of your old ideas, Vi," he explained. "You found a way of creating matter out of emptiness by solidifying the electronic orbits. I can reverse the process and so expand the electronic orbits that no matter worthy of the name remains. We'll have to act quickly, though, because the effect does not last beyond a few seconds."

He pressed the button. The beam from the instrument was invisible except as very faint green haze. Within its area the gleaming surface of the dome disappeared, leaving a gap. Immediately Abna stepped through it, helping the Amazon in after him. They had barely settled themselves on the ledge of rock immediately below the dome's rim before it began to reseal. Within a matter of seconds it was as solid as ever.

"The slight air escape and entry of ammonia is not sufficient to cause trouble," Abna said. "We can rid ourselves of our suits and get more freedom of movement."

In a moment or two they were free of the encumbrances, weapon belts about their waists. Though the Amazon felt hampered by her regal robes, she was ready for action nevertheless.

They started down the rocky slope of the enormous natural cavern, and it took them half an hour to complete the descent, which left them with quarter of a mile of level rock to cross before the city began.

"Well," the Amazon said, "how do we get to the surgical laboratory without getting blasted to pieces?"

Abna said: "I am still the ruler of Atlantis—the king of this city. I never relinquished that title, and my people were brought up to swear allegiance to their ruler."

"But you're supposed to be dead—and Quorne is completely in charge."

"During my absence, yes; I'm willing to gamble that most men in this city will obey me instead of him. If they won't do it willingly, I'll use mental compulsion. As for you, as my elected queen, they dare not touch you."

So with the complete assurance that he felt his position gave him, Abna began walking majestically across the rock area with the Amazon beside him. Her own step was defiant enough, but she kept a hand on her small protonic gun just the same.

They reached the main street of the city before they encountered anybody—then it was an Atlantean man just leaving the controlling headquarters.

He stopped when he saw Abna and the Amazon.

"Highness!" he gasped incredulously.

"Yes, my friend. I can imagine your surprise," Abna

replied. "Where is my adviser, Sefner Quorne?"

"His Excellency is in the surgery, highness," the man's eyes were round in wonder. "But, highness, it has been understood that you died. We buried you with ceremony and his Excellency took your place."

"I am aware of it. But I did not die—just a little joke of mine. I am holding you, my friend, to your original oath of allegiance—to serve me until death. That oath is also intended to embrace my wife here."

"You—you mean the Golden Amazon?"

"Since she is the only woman present—yes. Now take me to Quorne!"

"Yes, highness. Immediately."

The man turned and hurried on ahead. They ascended the broad steps of the controlling building together, and the guards in the corridor, evidently forewarned by the Atlantean moving on ahead, came to attention as the gigantic Abna passed them with the Amazon at his side. Their eyes strayed a little in profound wonder, but otherwise perfect respect was shown.

At the end of the vast corridor, so familiar to Abna from the days when he had ruled this region, the Atlantean stopped before a coppery-looking door and opened it. He said nothing to those inside.

Quorne turned casually, evidently expecting to see an Atlantean servant enter. He looked away, then back again sharply, his eyes fixed on Abna and the Amazon as they walked into the surgery.

Abna closed the door and came to a stop, the Amazon beside him.

"Stop the experiment," Abna commanded, looking at the surgeons, and for a moment they hesitated. Then at the grim light of compulsion in his eyes they stopped. Viona, still bound to the operating table, looked hopefully toward her father.

"You came just in time—both of you," she said.

"Silence!" Quorne barked at her; then he glared at the surgeons. "Continue! I will deal with this."

The surgeons failed to respond. They stood waiting.

"You seem to have forgotten, Quorne, that I am the ruler here," Abna said, stepping forward.

"You mean you were! I'm not trying to solve how you have come back from the dead and brought with you the Amazon, whom I also believed dead. The fact remains: I am the master of this city and only my orders will be obeyed."

Abna smiled a little. "Looks like it, doesn't it? Every man dashing to do your bidding!"

Quorne looked around him at the immovable surgeons and scientists. They were not exactly hypnotized, but they were certainly not exercising their own will.

Abna strode toward the operating table, and immediately Quorne stepped in front of him, his ray gun ready.

Abna lashed out his tremendous fist and sent Quorne reeling. He collapsed in a corner, his gun gone. He tried to get up, and then realized the Amazon was standing over him with her proton gun in her hand.

"You can stay there," she said bitterly, "until Abna

has decided what to do with you. If it were left to me, I would kill you this instant—as you killed me."

"The fact that you are here shows I did not kill you," Quorne snapped.

"But you did. How I returned to life is nobody's business except Abna's and my own."

The Amazon said no more. She divided her attention between the recumbent Quorne and Abna. In a matter of moments he had unfastened the straps holding Viona, cast away the electrodes with the suction cups, and then helped her to her feet. He handed her a spare gun. She nodded toward the nearby bath where a half-created image lay.

"Quorne had only got that far," she said, gripping Abna's arm. "You'd better undo his work; my gun is covering Quorne."

Abna nodded, and trained his weapon on the synthetic flesh. It vanished in cascades of light and a plume of smoke—then Abna strode through the fumes with Viona beside him and yanked the fallen Quorne to his feet.

"For you, Quorne, this is the finish." he said deliberately. "I shall not kill you because, having the scientific mind you have, you might find a way back and become a real menace. So as far as I am concerned, you can stay alive—but shorn of all power, outcast from every planet. You may collect whatever personal belongings you wish and then go."

"This is ridiculous, Abna!" the Amazon protested. "Destroy him!"

Abna shook his head. "You are too ruthless, Vi. It doesn't always pay."

Quorne left the surgery, and Abna said quietly: "There is nothing he can do, Vi. Everybody is with us now, not him.... Well, Viona, you don't seem very adept at taking care of yourself," he added, smiling—and the girl laughed.

"Perhaps not at taking care of myself, but I managed to queer things for Quorne. I smashed up his electro-magnetic rust business."

"So we noticed," the Amazon remarked. "For that you deserve congratulations."

"But not for anything else?" Viona asked in surprise.

"What, for instance?" The Amazon eyed her steadily. "You got yourself into a terrible tangle. Nor would you have escaped from it but for us."

"Your mother, too, has the habit of getting into deep water sometimes," Abna remarked. "That is when she finds me useful."

The Amazon looked at him indignantly, but before she could speak, Viona asked: "Father, does—does mother know? You've told her?"

"Everything. She has a daughter, but I haven't yet been able to find out whether she enjoys the fact or not."

"Of course I do." The Amazon relaxed for a moment and gave one of her rare smiles as she put an arm about the girl's shoulders. "And I'm sure that you'll be worthy of the name I have made throughout the system."

"I also have something to do with it—" Abna started

to say, then he paused and frowned. Something was happening.

It took him a few seconds to realize what it was—then he knew beyond doubt that he was mysteriously becoming bigger, and so was the Amazon beside him. Even in the brief time it took them to comprehend the fact, they had expanded upward and outward, to hear the scream of Viona in their ears. The vast expanse of the surgery became too small to them. It shrank as they struck the roof and passed through it—upward—outward.

They could not speak to each other. Ordinary emotions were wiped out. They were in the grip of a terrific magnetic power that paralyzed their movements. They saw the dome of the cavern coming to meet them, then they became suffused with a coruscating energy—

Had there been an observer, it would have seemed that they had utterly disappeared in a blinding explosion.

Abna and the Amazon found their senses reeling. They could no longer see or feel anything other than inchoate mental impressions. They were not breathing in the ordinary way; they were not even flesh-and-blood any more. Alarming, even terrifying mental impressions flooded their minds as they fought to make sense of what was happening to them. They had the impression that their bodies had swollen to such a gigantic size that they had become vastly attenuated gases, widely spread creatures of gyrating molecules and stretching electronic orbits.

They sensed that they were leaving Jupiter, travelling at a terrific, ever-increasing speed through space. Jupiter was only a globe to which they seemed to be vaguely connected. Jupiter was gone. Seemingly, they were moving at many times the speed of light, flashing outward toward Andromeda and leaving it behind. Out beyond the outposts of infinity, beyond the farthest barriers of the stars, to the very rim of the Universe.

They passed that, too. The sound of a million thunders seemed to explode around them as they shot beyond the rim of the molecule forming the known Universe. They were in a Universe beyond it.

Incapable of movement, or even thought, they lay flat on their backs, attuning themselves. Then gradually they noticed they were in the midst of a mossy green substance, as soft as velvet, while overhead in a near-purple sky there gyrated a binary sun of deep yellow—one small sun revolving around a much larger one. Evidently there was air, for they were breathing normally.

The Amazon moved slowly and then sat up. She was still dressed as she had been in the surgery—so was Abna. He rose beside her and they looked about them on the utterly deserted landscape. There was not a ridge, hollow, or irregularity anywhere. The gravity seemed to equal Earth's. The sky was incredible, apart from the binary sun. All the stars seemed to be double ones, and all moved with a noticeable rapidity. There was not a single constellation in the sky that was familiar.

"You realize what has happened?" Abna asked, getting to his feet and helping the Amazon rise.

"I can make a guess. We're in an utterly different solar system."

"Far more than that. We are in a different Universe!"

"But—that isn't possible."

"You know better, Vi. You are a scientist. The fact is that Quorne has performed a brilliant scientific feat which has ditched us more completely than anything that ever happened before."

"You mean," she said at last, "that Quorne had instruments in his laboratory that he turned on us?"

"He must have. Instruments tuned to our particular frequencies, which would not take him above a few seconds to get, since we were only a few yards away. He could work uninterrupted, since we didn't follow him. He must then have switched on twin vibratory beams that expanded the orbits of the electrons comprising our bodies. Didn't you sense that we were being expanded in size, Vi? Becoming so attenuated that we passed through the laboratory ceiling? "

The Amazon nodded, a look of utter bewilderment on her beautiful face. "The last thing I remember was the roof of the dome rushing to meet us, then there was a blinding flash and everything went hazy...." she shook her head irritably. "But such a thing can't have happened, Abna, or we would surely have died. If the orbits of the electrons forming our bodies had actually continued to get wider and wider, and we became correspondingly bigger, we'd simply have became a gas, our molecules spread out, and all our life and consciousness would have been blasted from us. We couldn't have continued expanding into another universe—once we got beyond the dome, our atoms would simply have become swallowed up in the hurricane winds of the Jovian atmosphere!"

"I agree—and that was almost certainly Quorne's intention. But we *didn't* get beyond the dome, Vi," Abna pointed out. "Remember that blinding flash? The energies Quorne had infused into our bodies must have reached some kind of critical mass. They punched a hole through the fabric of space, and that was when we made the transition from our universe into another dimension entirely. That saved us, and it was something that Quorne did not foresee. "

"I had a weird sensation that I was hurtling through space faster than light," the Amazon murmured. "Surely that couldn't have happened?"

"I felt the same thing," Abna admitted. "But that was simply our subconscious mind trying to make sense of what was happening to us. What actually happened is that we were forced outside the fabric of our own space-time and through other dimensions, and when the energy dissipated itself and the limit of extension was reached, we burst through the molecule comprising our Universe, and emerged into this greater molecule, this macrocosm beyond. Somewhere in infinity is one molecule—and tens of thousands of them can cluster on the head of a pin—in which lies a Universe. And in that Universe is Earth, Jupiter, all the known planets and constellations. To them we are Colossi—and we have no knowledge of how to get home."

The Amazon said no word. Even her vast imagination was stunned by the fact that the Universe-bubble could be broken through, to give entrance to the greater Universe beyond. And now? Only this emptiness, this soft carpet that seemed to cover the planet. No wind. No sound. Gentle warmth from the double sun. Once in her experience, when she had been flung far beyond the solar system, the Amazon had felt fear; and she felt it again now. Her hand closed on Abna's mighty arm.

"You have the mastery over matter, Abna," she said, looking at him intently. "Can't you think of a way out of this?"

"Not immediately. Our distance from home is approximately twenty-seven, followed by twenty-seven noughts, expressible in light centuries. It is inconceivable, even to me. I can't work out the mathematics. We're right beyond our Universe."

"And Viona," the Amazon muttered, remembering the despairing cry she had heard.

"She must be fighting alone," Abna replied. "We cannot aid her— And there is a more disquieting thought, too. Since we have become so vast, and our normal field of activity is so small by comparison, it means that time here is moving far more slowly than it will be on Jupiter. A second here may be a century on Jupiter. It is possible that by now hundreds of years have passed."

Abna became silent, realizing what his statement

meant. It implied that Viona might already be aged nearly to the point of death, unless the vast changes of events and domination of Quorne had killed her long since.

"Abna, there's got to be a way back!"

He did not respond. He was busy exerting his tremendous mentality to get to grips with the problem—but the equations would not balance; the integrals were out of line. Then as he pondered, a change came over the face of things. A peculiar forked shadow moved across the purple sky and grew larger. It finally seemed to fill all space. The Amazon drew closer to Abna, waiting anxiously, then she cried out a little as the shadow actually gripped her tightly about the waist and raised her. Abna, too, was raised beside her and both of them performed a dizzying arc through space.

They finished the crazy flight by lying on their backs, and the black shadow moved away. The sky seemed unchanged. The gyrating double sun was still there, and so were the stars. But there was also penetrating light pouring down on them in a single blinding ray from an infinite distance. To look at it was impossible, so they jerked their heads away and instead studied the queer, smooth stone on which they were lying. The mossy plain had disappeared.

Then something as large as an oval spaceship was lying beside them. It looked like a huge animal—no, a slug. It had hair as thick as rope.

"It's—a finger!" the Amazon cried, astounded, staring at it. "Now I understand; we are infinitely tiny, having burst from a molecular state, and around us are beings who, by comparison, are stupendously big."

Abna turned his head and, shading his eyes from the glare, tried to gaze into remoteness. There were far-away twinkling stars now, and something as dark as Cygnus moving in the backdrop.

"This is tile we're lying on," the Amazon added. "That other stuff was not a planet after all, but a round ball of some kind— Now what?" She broke off in alarm, as a convulsive tension seized her body.

Abna did not answer. The sense of paralysis was too intense. He lay in breathless wonder watching the swirling change of his surroundings. The face of things was gyrating, enlarging, assuming meaning. Gigantic instruments became smaller. The stars became larger and assumed the position of normal lights in a ceiling. The double sun decreased to a single-bright globe, while underneath it was spinning an air-cooling fan that, by continuity of vision, had given the impression of a small sun circling a big one.

Normalcy. With a queer little jerk the paralysis ceased. Abna and the Amazon found themselves still lying on white tile beneath a gigantic horseshoe magnet apparatus in a laboratory.

# CHAPTER NINE
## A WAY TO KILL

They got to their feet, with their eyes fixed on a small being no larger than three feet tall, yet with legs nearly as thick as his body. His huge head was totally bald. Tiny eyes peered from the enormous cranium. Then as he moved it became apparent that his gigantic head was actually supported by a cage-like affair that rested on his shoulders.

"Weight of knowledge, I hope," Abna commented, and almost immediately he nearly reeled by the terrific impact of thought waves which came from the being.

"I welcome you, my friends—" The waves paused and were modified, just as a yelling voice might drop to normal. "I am sorry. I had forgotten for the moment I was not conversing with one of my learned colleagues. They are usually so absorbed in their thoughts one has to concentrate with extreme violence to penetrate their consciousness."

Abna stepped forward and took the little being's hand, shaking it warmly. The action seemed to surprise the creature, then evidently by thought reading he understood it was a sign of greeting.

"Thank heaven, we landed among scientists," Abna said eagerly. "This is my—"

"Yes, yes. I understand. Your mate. Wife, as you call it.... You have come a vastly long distance, my friends. Even my mind reels as I try to compute the mathematics. I would say a distance of eight by nine plus quadrillion plus quintillion light centuries. Infinite expansion outward from the parent molecule. Very extraordinary. Very interesting."

"We have to get back!" the Amazon insisted. "Much though we would like to stay here and exchange scientific notes, it is imperative we return before too much time has gone by. A second here may be a century in our universe."

"True," the being admitted.

"I beg of you to understand," Abna said earnestly. "I do not need to explain the situation: you can read it all from my mind. How do we return home?"

"That is problematical. I am Tarnec Brodix, a master mathematician. You are Abna and Amazon. I greet you. This world is Mil-256, one of a series of 256 planets revolving round a primary. We live underground. More peaceful."

The stabbing, brief thoughts ceased for a moment and then resumed.

"You burst your molecule and arrived here—on the felt knob of one of those canisters there. I happened to notice you, lifted you with forceps to an enlarging equipment, and here you are."

The Amazon was becoming irritated. "Tarnec

Brodix, please understand us! Please! The time is flying by. The safety of worlds is endangered with every moment we are absent. We—"

"You are scientists. You can master some forms of matter by thought. We never achieved that art. In fact, we do not need to. We are master mathematicians."

"We must go home. I cannot master this problem." Abna admitted. "Can you, with your mathematical genius?"

Tarnec Brodix seemed to relapse into a trance. Odd snatches of his thoughts floated to the desperately anxious pair.

"...the fifth integral. The quotient placed at the root of the ninteenth pyramid, producing the double angle which in turn is reflected by the triple ramification of the seventeenth dimension...." The mastermind went on, absorbed in his problem. Then he added rationally: "I cannot see any real purpose will have been served if you go back, my friends. It will mean 5,000 years have passed. That is, even if you went now—which you will not."

"Five thousand years!" the Amazon echoed in horror.

"The microcosmic and macrocosmic times are entirely different in ratio," Tarnec Brodix explained.

"Five thousand years or otherwise, is there a way back?" Abna demanded.

"Yes. But you have not the intelligence to grasp it. You can only get back if I take you."

"Which, as a scientist, you will," the Amazon said. "We got here through no fault of our own and, wonderful though this meeting is with a being of another Universe, we—"

"Pardon me," came the thoughts of the super-brain. "I must retire and meditate."

Abna, horrified at the thought of the flying minutes and corresponding centuries, started to protest. It was quite useless. The being mysteriously vanished into thin air and the complicated laboratory was deserted.

"Urgency is one thing he does not appreciate," she said.

"Possibly because he can make time obey him. When you have mastered time and space, as he seems to have done, there is no need for urgency in anything. Nothing we can do but wait for him to come back, I suppose."

"In spite of everything, this experience is unique," the Amazon said, reflecting. "To meet the beings of other worlds is something which has always fascinated me. All so different to ourselves. But this creature is by far the cleverest—and the most absent-minded—I ever encountered."

"Just take a look at this city!" Abna cried, and the Amazon turned to find he was standing at a window.

She gazed out in amazement. Of all the strange places she had ever seen in her varied experiences, this was the strangest. It was bizarre, the apparent creation of a nightmare. Every building was different in design and, in bulk, the edifices covered a seemingly limitless distance. They did not vanish over the horizon in the ordinary way; instead, they shaded off into a queer blur which gave the impression of looking at a titanic horizontal V, viewing it from base to apex. Some of the buildings were cubes, others were oblongs, some circular.

In the air there moved vague mathematical postulations, taking shape for a moment and then disappearing. Somewhere there was a sun. Its light was visible, but not the source.

"A mathematical planet," Abna said, even his far-reaching knowledge overpowered. "I often wondered if such a thing could exist—if mathematics could be brought to such a point that nothing else existed."

"If you hadn't created a daughter for us and given us need to return hone, we could spend the rest of our lives here solving problems," the Amazon mused, her eyes wistful for a moment. "As it is—"

She paused. Tarnec Brodix had returned.

"Meditation is complete," he announced in his queer, jerky thought waves. "I will return you to your space and, if equations balance, to your own time. I am doing it because I enjoy trying to reverse time and abbreviate space. It is a problem in ninety-seven dimensions, something I have long wanted to try."

Abna and the Amazon glanced at each other. At the most they understood the fourth dimension and had vague gleanings about the fifth.

"When do we go?" Abna asked urgently.

"Within a few moments. I must create our vehicle."

"You mean a spaceship, or atom ship?" the Amazon inquired.

The bald head shook briefly in its cage. "Neither. We shall wrap ourselves in a cocoon of figurations. Come over here."

Tarnec Brodix paused in the midst of a floor made up of thousands of different sections, every one mathematical, and reflecting light in a myriad of different ways. Overhead, perhaps ten feet above, were two vast rods that nearly touched at their lower pointed extremities. They were connected to a switch panel that was the last word in complication.

Brodix said: "We are standing on an equational mosaic. It is composed of what we call mathematical variants, which can be reacted upon by the arithmetical essences directed from these two dimensional extensions overhead. I close the switch and we become enveloped in mathematical vibrations. If my calculations are correct—and I am incapable of error—we shall be transported from this macro-universe into your smaller micro-universe."

The mastermind's tiny hand moved a switch—and immediately extraordinary phenomena took place. Pale walls with pronounced curvature sprang out of nowhere and enclosed the three on the mosaic plate. They could see through the barrier, but the view was limited to darkness with one or two gyrating stars.

Presently, however, as the incredible apparatus of the pure mathematician expanded into full power, there began to appear through the walls the swirling immensities of space.

None of it was recognizable to the Amazon or

Abna. Indeed, it changed so swiftly there was not the time for identification. They saw—or thought they saw—nebulae, swirling pools of utter dark, the haze of skimming suns, the twirling beauty of magnificent star clusters, and all the time they both kept trying to fathom where they themselves were. They seemed to be still standing on their mathematical floor, the tiny, big-headed master mind at work on his switchboard.

"I sense you are hungry." Brodix said. "We never eat. In mathematics we have life."

Light without source glowed on the weird instruments. The two-dimensional bars still projected downward, their lengths transformed by an illusory impression of rippling colours. Then Brodix turned, his tiny eyes shadowed by his mighty cranium.

"Calculations complete," he announced. "We shall be reintegrated through ninety-seven dimensions into a master pattern. When that reintegration is complete, we shall be on the planet you call Jupiter, in the midst of a city under a dome—which I gather from your thoughts is your wish."

"But what of the passage of time?" the Amazon asked in anxiety. "If thousands of years have passed—"

"Time is but a progression through space involving other dimensions. In mathematics one can curve around a progressive forward movement and come back to an earlier point. I have allowed for time movement. You will reintegrate at a point advanced exactly twelve hours from the period when you departed."

"Only a day—Earth time—will have passed?"

Abna cried. "Brodix, if there is ever anything we can do which will help you, you have but to ask! You don't know what this means to us."

The mastermind was unmoved by gratitude, or any other emotion. He was as impersonal as the figures he controlled.

"The problem has interested me. I shall return home when the reintegration is complete, and brood for many cycles on the thing I have accomplished." The thoughts changed. "This Sefner Quorne. He hinders you. Do you wish I should translate him?

"Translate him?" the Amazon repeated hazily.

"It is the supreme punishment. Those of our race who make mistakes are translated. They are converted into a mathematical postulation, left free to wander in time trying to seek completion. But they cannot. One figure in the total calculation is omitted, so completeness can never be achieved. It is anguish. Eternal striving to become whole again—which can never happen without the missing figure."

"Sounds diabolical," Abna muttered. "And who has the missing figure? You?"

"Yes. Or whoever has created the postulation."

The Amazon's violet eyes were glowing.

"There couldn't be anything better for Quorne—turned loose in space, unable to understand what has beaten him. I like the idea immensely."

The mastermind brooded for a while, then his thoughts came again. "This Quorne has no entanglements whom you wish to preserve? I refer to progenitors or anybody of that nature. In working out the mathematical sequences which must dissolve him, the pattern is bound to involve all who are in his mathematical orbit—progenitors, brothers, sisters, and so forth."

"You can go right ahead, Brodix." the Amazon responded. "I don't think Quorne has any relatives, but even if he has, they might as well be destroyed with him."

"So be it," the mastermind responded.

Tarnec Brodix had not made any mistake. Though neither the Amazon nor Abna had any idea how long their astounding transition from the Great to the Small took, they were aware of transformations in the face of things when Brodix finally announced they were not far from the journey's end.

Out of the chaos of whirling stars and nebulae, outside solidity took shape. Instrument panels came into view, vast girders supporting a roof. Enormous scientific engines. Men moving. A slender girl in their midst. All of them were motionless, watching fixedly a phenomenon taking place in the very air before them.

The imprisoning walls of equational variants disappeared and the Amazon, Abna, and Brodix found themselves gazing at Viona, Quorne, and the men of Atlantis. They were in the huge laboratory from which Quorne handled his scientific schemes.

For a long minute there was an astounded silence, then Viona gave a desperate cry of relief and raced across the intervening space.... Quorne ran after her, only to stop in his tracks and crash on his face as he struck an invisible barrier.

"Mother—father—!" Viona caught at them tightly. For once in her young life she was obviously frightened, her blue eyes wide, her slender body trembling. "I—I never thought I'd see you again."

"Get up, Quorne!" Abna commanded, striding forward after he had embraced Viona.

"Wait!" commanded the thoughts of Brodix, and Abna paused.

The mastermind moved slowly on his blocks of legs, his queer hypertrophied head wagging in the midst of the cage support. Quorne, dishevelled and bewildered, slowly groped his way to his feet. He knew as he stared at the tiny man of a far-flung universe that here was something far beyond his ken—a being of pure figures, unemotional, ruthless, concerned only with the absolute correctness of mathematics.

"You are Quorne," Brodix's thoughts snapped. "I have decided on your dissolution from the scheme of things. You have considerable, but not great, scientific knowledge—and you perpetually abuse it. No system, no universe, has any place for such a being."

"Stop him!" Quorne shouted hoarsely, looking across at the Amazon and Abna. "This battle between us is ours alone. It doesn't involve a creature like this. It—"

Quorne did not have the chance to say any more. Under the terrific onslaught of the mastermind's mathematical thoughts, he found himself mysteriously becoming transparent. He gave a final desperate cry for help and then disappeared.

Stunned with amazement, the remaining men toward the rear of the laboratory stared blankly at the space where their master had been.

"An interesting problem," Tarnec Brodix commented, returning slowly to the Amazon, Abna and Viona. "I wish you well, my friends. I shall brood on this for cycles to come."

"We can't thank you enough," Abna said, gripping the queer shoulders. "It's wonderful to know that such super intelligence exists, even if they are in a universe beyond our own."

"Time and space are all one," Brodix answered, then he stepped on to the vaguely visible mathematical mosaic on the floor. There was a brief gleam of inexplicable colours and he had gone.

To assimilate the situation demanded several moments, then, while the Amazon took charge of the girl, Abna strode across to the scientists.

"What is the situation?" he demanded. "On what kind of a scheme was Quorne engaged? How far had he got with his synthetic double experiment?"

"He had completed the experiment, highness," one of the men hurried to answer. "The doubles are in the surgical laboratory and—"

"Destroy them!" Abna interrupted, and the man departed hurriedly to obey the order. Then Abna turned to the remaining men. "Whether or not you will die for serving a traitor like Quorne depends upon my generosity," he said curtly. "You can help yourselves by telling me exactly what Quorne did during the time my wife and I were forced to be absent."

"Much of it we did not see, highness," one of the men replied. "But he made us complete the repairs to the electromagnetic machinery."

Abna looked in the direction of the huge wire matrix as the Atlantean glanced toward it.

"It is not in operation," the man added. "His excellency was just on the point of restoring it to activity when you reappeared."

"Destroy it," Abna ordered. "All of you use your ray guns on it."

He stood watching as the wonder mesh of wires and instrumentation was smashed for the second time. Then he looked toward the Amazon and Viona.

"From here on, I am restoring the old rulership, Vi," he said, returning to them. "These Atlanteans will obey my commands from now on, which means that Jupiter and the moons you've made habitable can become a useful stopping place for inner-planet space machines on their way to the outer planets. This city here, under its protective dome, is now controlled by you and me, in the name of Earth and the inner planets. Agreed?"

"Certainly," the Amazon responded. "And what about Saturn?"

"That world is ours," Abna answered. "Yours, Viona's, and mine. The world to where we can retire when we wish to be peaceful and think out our own particular problems. It is to remain forever inviolate.

The conditions of Saturn seem particularly suitable for mental creation—as witness the city of Millennia."

"And the planets as yet untouched?" the Amazon inquired. "There is no point in making this world of Jupiter a stopping place for fliers on their way to the outer worlds, if none of them has yet been taken over. We have still to know what Uranus and Neptune contain. Pluto we have already visited, and can discount it as worthless rock."

"Uranus and Neptune can be next on our plans of exploration," Abna said.

Two hours later, refreshed and rested, the Amazon Abna and Viona were in the private suite that had formerly belonged to Quorne. It was clear from Abna's expression that he had a good deal on his mind.

"Nothing would please me better than to retire to Millennia and there devote my time to scientific problems along with you, Vi—but unfortunately, we have lesser mortals to consider. Earth and Mars, according to the latest radio reports I have received, are in a pretty bad state. Everything is in a state of collapse after Quorne's activities. We made a mistake in having Brodix dissolve him before we had found out the neutralizing agent. So we must discover it for ourselves."

"There are thousands of projectiles stored away in the laboratories," Viona remarked. "They are filled with nitrine fluid, the stuff that causes the rusting. I see no reason why we can't analyze it and find its opposite number."

"The only way," the Amazon agreed. "Once we have that, we shall have to help the inner worlds to restore their shattered cities. It may take a year, two years, for them to do it—but we don't need to stay with them that long. There are capable engineers on all the worlds."

Abna smiled. "You are thinking Vi, as I am, that it is time we withdrew from the affairs of the inner planets and let them handle things in their own way?"

"We do not think as they do," the Amazon shrugged. "You and I have our own lives to lead, our own scientific explorations to make. With Quorne removed, no danger remains in the system. Besides, we also need time in which to instruct Viona here in the arts of science. Before she again flies about the cosmos on her own, she needs considerable instruction."

Viona did not say anything. She was seated in a chair, considering the floor moodily.

"Anything the matter, Viona?" Abna asked, going over to her and putting an arm about her shoulders.

"Matter?" She looked up sharply, a look that was almost fear in her blue eyes for a moment. "No, why should there be?"

"You are unusually quiet, that's all. As a rule your high spirits are something of a problem, but you have not smiled once since your mother and I returned. If Quorne is on your mind, or you haven't recovered from your ordeal at his hands, try and realize the fact that he has gone forever and can never come back."

"What actually happened to Quorne?" she asked.

"He became an incomplete equation and can never

achieve unity without the missing factor. The missing factor is in the control of Brodix—the mastermind whom you saw. The matter of Quorne is out of our hands. He is somewhere in space and time, a lost entity."

Viona was silent, reflecting, a curious look in her eyes. The Amazon moved across to her.

"What is the matter?" she asked. "I suppose your mind could be read if necessary—"

"No, it couldn't!" Viona interrupted, looking up in sudden anger. "I can defend myself against that."

"Neither your father nor I would ever do that," the Amazon said, surprised.

Viona got to her feet and began to pace the room. At last she seemed to make up her mind, and faced them.

"I was a much bigger failure in my fight against Quorne than either of you realize!" Her voice was bitter with self-reproach. "I don't know how you're going to take this. Quorne will never he dead as long as there remains the possibility of his offspring being born."

Abna glanced at the Amazon sharply.

"Meaning?" The Amazon's face was expressionless.

"You heard the Atlanteans say that Quorne completed his synthesis experiments? He did—making hundreds of images of me for intended distribution to the men of this city. Progeny would have followed—but Quorne reserved me, the original, for himself. He made me go through the ceremony of marriage. I had no means of defending myself. I was drugged, hypnotized...."
Viona's rising voice stopped suddenly, then in a half

sullen tone she added: "I am the wife of Quorne!"

The unspoken implication was immediately obvious to the Amazon. She hesitated over saying something. She was taken utterly off guard.

"So you see, Quorne is not dead," Viona said. "A legacy of him is left behind. I'm going to have his child."

The Amazon flashed an anxious glance at Abna. "Can you picture the child of Quorne? His evil genius, perhaps, and our science. Such a child might become a worse problem than any we have ever known! We'll have to have it—"

Viona's lips tightened. "It's my child—not yours!" she snapped. "I'm having it, and you'd better not try to stop me!"

The Amazon relaxed a little and put an arm about Viona's shoulders.

"You did well to tell us. But think what it means! Think what a complete victory it will be for the cult of Quorne if, through you, he leaves behind a factor so brilliant and deadly that we cannot stand against it!"

"And the problem does not end there," Abna mused.

The Amazon and Viona glanced at him quickly.

Abna said: "I am thinking of Brodix. Remember what he said about all things within Quorne's mathematical orbit being dissolved with him?"

"Yes, but surely that referred to blood relations?" the Amazon asked quickly. "Besides, Viona was not affected when Quorne was wiped out. I don't see how she can be now."

"What did you mean about my being in Quorne's mathematical orbit?" Viona asked.

"It is hard to explain," Abna mused over it for a moment. "Probably it doesn't signify. Brodix implied that anybody in Quorne's orbit—a relation that is— would be dissolved with him when he became an incomplete equation. Since nothing has affected you, we can be pretty certain that nothing will."

"I see." Tight-lipped, Viona left the room.

"A legacy indeed!" Abna muttered fiercely. "Something we never bargained for!"

"One day," the Amazon said slowly, "we shall perhaps realize that Quorne is a menace dead or alive. However, there is nothing we can do about it, though we must certainly be on our guard in the years to come. I think we had better get some of that nitrine fluid and analyze it."

She moved to the door, and in a few moments had traversed the corridor to the main laboratory.

# CHAPTER TEN
## VANISHING LADY

From the Atlanteans gathered there, she learned where the nitrine fluid projectiles were stored, and before very long was deep in analysis. The scientific preoccupation helped to keep her mind away from the problem of Viona. She had been making tests for nearly an hour when Abna joined her.

"Learned anything?" he questioned.

"I think so." The Amazon straightened up. "I've just made the final reaction tests. I know now what nitrine is. Basically, it is a disintegrative powder made from heavy water, much as brine is a deposit of seawater. The best nullification for it lies in this extract of copper-x crystals. They absorb the liquid and convert it into vapour, which prevents it having any effect. It is similar to preventing metal rusting by having it heated, so water settling upon it is converted into steam."

The Amazon demonstrated with the copper-x crystals, and it was obvious that upon them the nitrine fluid had no effect.

"Seems decisive," Abna agreed. "The best thing to do is have the scientists of Earth and the colonists on

Mars duplicate this copper-x solution immediately. They can prevent the progressive rusting that way, and start to rebuild. Let me have the complete formula."

The Amazon handed it over, then said: "I don't think we are doing very wisely leaving the scientists of those worlds to work things out for themselves. They have not our experience. I suggest that you go to Mars and supervise. I will go to the Moon, and Viona can go to Earth. Each one of us will take a formula. Agreed?"

"But why not send Viona to the Moon?" Abna asked. "There's only a small domed colony there."

"I want to see how the lunar colony is progressing, and if it can be extended. It's a long time since I visited the Moon to check on things. Besides, it will show Viona that we have faith in her abilities."

"Yes, it's the best way," Abna assented. "When that job is done, we'll return here, have the Jovian system converted into a fuelling centre, and then we'll retire to Millennia and work out the details of our Uranus and Neptune expeditions."

He lost no time in having three space ships prepared; then by radio he informed the controllers of the inner worlds of his intentions. Viona, summoned to hear of the plan, accepted her particular assignment without argument.

"How long you will have to remain on Earth to supervise depends on how quickly the Earth engineers get things under control," the Amazon explained. "You can consider it your first important assignment."

Viona's face began to brighten a little. "Which

means that you and father still have faith in me?"

"Of course!" Abna exclaimed. "We know your capabilities—and your failings. This job should give you the chance of finding out the difficulties you will have to master later. If you get into any trouble, you can always reach your mother or me by radio. While on Earth, you will stay with Chris Wilson's family, whom you already know."

So, her instructions completed, Viona set out for Earth an hour later in her superfast flyer. Abna and the Amazon departed a little while afterwards in separate machines, leaving behind them orders for the Atlanteans to commence the dismantling of all scientific apparatus and prepare to build a vast fuelling station under the dome instead. The power and the glory assembled in the buried city was to be no more. That lay in Millennia.

Viona reached Earth safely and immediately sought out Chris Wilson at his London home. Fortunately, the residence was made of old-fashioned brick arid timber, and so had escaped the ravages of metal destruction.

When Viona outlined the neutralizing plan to him, he summoned leading engineers, and every available laboratory was set to work on the manufacture of copper-x crystals. These were crushed into a fine powder and then sprayed from thousands of aircraft, until not a square inch of Earth's surface had been left untouched. The scheme worked to perfection. The disintegration of metal ceased, and the new ingots coming from the foundries—blazing away day and night—remained solid and uncorroded. Rebuilding began.

Absorbed in watching order come gradually out of chaos, and proud of the fact that she offered endless valuable scientific suggestions, Viona failed to notice certain changes taking place within herself. But Chris did, and spoke about them to his wife. At first they thought that perhaps the girl was run down from the enormous efforts she had been making, until the absurdity of it because obvious. The child of Abna and the Amazon could not possibly suffer from such a condition. No, it was something else.

The change in Viona took the form of a curious delicacy of outline. From being a virile young woman full of bounding energy, she became in three months more ethereal. Her skin lost its copper-bronze tint and became waxen.

The biggest shock of all came in the fourth month. It happened one morning when Chris was in the big Central London control office studying the new building plans with Viona at his side. As her hand reached out to indicate a certain point he noticed that he could see through her hand. He tried to think it was a trick of the light; then, when he realized it was not, he swung on the girl sharply.

Her startled blue eyes met his. She, too, had seen the phenomenon at the same moment. Raising her hand, she held it to the light. It was as transparent as glass. Lifting the other hand beside it she found it normal.

"Tarnec Brodix," she whispered; then without

explaining further she snapped on the intercom. Her voice was agitated as she spoke to the control operator. "Get me my father right away," she ordered. "Red City—Mars."

After the usual delay, the radio wave reached Mars and communication was established. Her words almost tumbling over one another, Viona explained the situation. Her last sentences betrayed that fear, that quality so latently developed in her makeup, was beginning to gain a hold.

"What do I do?" she entreated. "I keep thinking of that weird creature Tarnec Brodix and what he said about people with Quorne being involved."

An agonizing wait whilst the radio waves crossed the interplanetary gulf, then:

"Set off into space immediately," Abna told her. "I will do likewise and ask your mother to join me. We'll meet halfway. That will cut down time. It seems as though only mind force over matter can put you straight. Leave immediately. Chris will be able to manage things now. All right, Viona—we'll join you in space."

Chris looked at Viona sympathetically as the visor screen went blank. "This is the queerest thing I ever struck. What is it exactly? A sort of invisibility disease?"

"No—mathematics." Viona replied briefly. "Goodbye, Chris."

She hurried out. By the time her fast flyer was climbing into space, her hand had become even more transparent, an effect which was noticeable as far as her elbow. Her fears for herself deepened when, just after she had left Earth's outermost rim of atmosphere, her hand and arm vanished entirely from the elbow. Yet she still had normal feeling in her fingers, for she held the switches.

She had no sense of discomfort; only a deep, profound worry. She gave her machine every scrap of power. No further changes had occurred in her by when she saw two space machines coming to meet her. She lowered the vacuum trap, which fixed itself to the airlock of her machine on the outside—then, no air escaping, the other end of the trap fastened to Abna's vessel, and then to the Amazon's. Before very long they were both in the control room. They gazed in startled wonder at Viona's troubled young face and then at the left arm truncated from the elbow.

"It's still there," Viona said. "It just isn't visible."

"Brodix was right," Abna said. "It's the only answer, but it has taken some time, evidently, for the necessary mathematics involved to work out. Mind should master matter. I will try, as never before. Lie down, Viona. Exert no mental effort. Put your mind completely at rest."

Viona did as she had been ordered, settling on the wall bed. Abna remained standing, studying her fixedly, his clenched hands and the taut veins in his massive neck showing the immense mental power he was exerting. The Amazon said nothing. She watched anxiously. Drops of perspiration appeared on Abna's forehead.

A change came to Viona, but not in the way he had expected. She became transparent across the face and where her bare throat and shoulders lay. It was possible to see the cushions through them.

Abna relaxed, bitter regret on his features.

"I cannot do it," he said, his voice low. "This new spread of transparency proves me powerless. The force of assembled mathematics is too great for my mind control to deal with. I'm fighting the whole Universe when it comes to figures, chiefly because the Universe itself is an equation, perfectly balanced—"

He broke off and the Amazon gave a little gasp. Abruptly Viona's transparency took on complete nothingness. She vanished utterly, leaving behind slowly crumpling clothes.

The shock was tremendous. It left the Amazon and Abna gazing in speechless dismay. They moved around uselessly for a while, whipping up the empty clothes, searching the space machine, calling Viona by name. At last Abna turned a drawn face.

"We're wasting time," he said. "Mathematical variants have worked themselves out, and dissolved Viona with them. Our only possible way to ever locate Viona again is to find Brodix."

"But how can we? He's somewhere in a universe beyond ours. We've no possible means of finding a way to him."

"Not physically," Abna admitted. "We might mentally. It is our only chance. We must go to Millennia immediately. It is the only place where absolutely peaceful concentration can be obtained."

He swung to the airlock, cast off the vacuum trap, and then slammed over the heavy operculum. Moving to the control board, he sent a radio message to Earth giving the position of the two abandoned spaceships so that they could be picked up, then started to build up power at the fastest possible speed.

In their time the Amazon and Abna had both made space journeys at tremendous speeds, but never so fast as now. Abna had the lever in top notch within a matter of thirty minutes, and the resultant terrific acceleration forced him and the Amazon down to the floor and held them there, the automatic devices taking care of the piloting.

At almost the speed of light they hurtled onward straight through the asteroid belt with repeller shields at maximum, and even so took numberless heavy impacts from the whirling meteorites and rocks. Then on towards Jupiter. He was bypassed and the void to Saturn became clear. Abna slowed down somewhat because of the necessity of mastering the vagaries of the planet's rings—which he accomplished successfully.

When the vessel dropped through the Saturnian cloud belts and came to rest on the rocky plain, which, to the Amazon, was vaguely familiar, it surprised her how, by an effort of mental power, Abna had changed the exterior conditions. Green fields, a ball of energy for a sun, and not very far away, the amethyst city.

"Saturn is definitely a world whereon mental effort brings an immediate and rich reward," he said. "Must be something in its constitution. It is not nearly so simple on other planets."

He opened the airlock, and with the Amazon beside him made his way to Millennia's magnificent main street. The whole city, though a product of materialized thought waves, had all the solidity of before. It was real, tangible, and magnificent. It gave the troubled Amazon the vague hope that within its sanctuary a way might be found to contact that mind of minds, Tarnec Brodix.

Once within the building that he had reserved for himself and the Amazon, Abna paused only long enough to provide refreshments for both of them. Then he settled down to a long spell of concentration trying with all the strength of his mind to reach out across the known Universe and contact that other being so inconceivably far away.

The Amazon did her utmost to help. But nothing came of their efforts. Not the faintest glimmer in their consciousness appeared to show that perhaps Brodix, somewhere, had understood.

"Wait!" Suddenly Abna leaped to his feet. "Vi, there is one possibility which we have overlooked. When Quorne sent us into the super universe, he used instruments in the Atlantis laboratory. We have never bothered to look at them or for them. If dismantling has not gone too far, they might still be there, their controls set exactly as they were when we were projected. If so, and we could use the same exact direction and vibration again, we would surely arrive within range of Tarnec Brodix's world."

"It's worth a try," the Amazon agreed, and almost before she had finished speaking, Abna had rushed out of the room and into the laboratory to use the short-wave radio equipment.

By the time the Amazon had caught up with him he had established contact with the chief laboratory technician of Jupiter, and she was just in time to hear his response to Abna's urgent question.

"No, highness, not all the laboratory equipment has yet been dismantled," he replied. "If you wish, I will hold up the demolition for the moment."

"Do that," Abna confirmed. "I am leaving for Atlantis immediately."

He switched off and the Amazon did not need to ask questions. She had gathered the drift, and followed him out to their space machine. Millennia vanished into thin air as Abna's thought waves cancelled it out of being; then the machine was hurtling into the Saturnian tempests.

At the fastest possible speed, Abna covered the distance to Jupiter, the safety trap in the giant dome opening before his urgent radio signals. Consumed with only one thought, he and the Amazon hurried to the great laboratory, each of them commencing a search of the regions which so far had been untouched. The Amazon was the first to locate the urgently wanted apparatus.

"Here it is!" she exclaimed, and Abna came hurrying

over to her.

Together they studied the projector instrument, which, their scientific knowledge told them, must have been the one Quorne had used. It had twin projection lenses. To them was geared a detector device by which objects at a distance could be easily identified by the aura.

"This is it," the Amazon insisted. "And look at this range setting. It's on infinity—which maybe accounts for the dimensional warp that caused us to burst free of this Universe bubble completely."

Abna nodded absently and the Amazon gave him a quick look.

"Why the delay?" she asked impatiently. "I'm willing to take the chance of making the journey again if it brings us within range of Brodix."

"It probably will not," Abna answered, "because space is constantly changing position. The Universe revolves around a common hub in relation to the extra universes outside it. We might take a risk that would be the end of us—for without the help of Brodix we could never come back.... No, I've a better plan. Let us record a spoken account of our troubles and send that to him in the macro-universe. He read our minds and so will be able to understand the words. We will enclose it in a highly magnetic casing that will be bound to affect Brodix's instruments if it arrives anywhere near him. The rest we can leave to him. He'll know what to do."

The Amazon saw the wisdom of the sugges-tion. Moving to the sound recording equipment, she checked that it was ready. Abna came over to her, switched on, and raised the microphone. He described in detail exactly what had occurred, during which time the Amazon was busy magnetizing a copper case that would carry the recording on its inconceivable journey. The finished message was sealed in the container and then put within range of one of the projector lenses. The moment the beam touched it that expansion of electronic orbits began.

The copper case became larger and still larger. In time it filled half the laboratory; then three-quarters, but since its expansion of size also thinned its material texture, it did not smash any of the surrounding machines. Instead it passed through them, as tenuous as a gas.

Larger and yet larger, the Amazon and Abna watching in fascinated silence, then Abna snapped: "Better look away now, Vi!" Seconds later there was a blinding flash as the cylinder vanished into a dimensional warp.

Abna turned to the Amazon. "Nothing more we can do now but hope for the best," he said. "And that is going to be the hardest job of all."

To Abna and the Amazon the hours seemed endless as they waited in the suite in the main building of Atlantis. They spoke but little, too preoccupied, nor did they concern themselves with the activities of the Atlanteans who went on with the task of dismantling all dangerous instruments save the vital one for the control of atomic orbits.

Refreshment—uneasy slumber—more waiting. Days and nights drifted by and nothing happened.

"Maybe we should have gone ourselves, after all," Abna commented at last when approximately four days and nights of Earth time had gone by. "Brodix would surely have done something by now if he had received our message."

"I'm going to try to reassemble that reflective planetoid," the Amazon decided, getting to her feet. "I've been thinking a good deal about it and I don't see why, with magnetic beams, I can't draw the scattered particles together again and weld them into a complete whole. It would mean a thought amplification of thousands of times normal. Brodix might then be able to detect it."

"I suppose it's worth a try," Abna admitted. "I have another suggestion, though. Suppose just one of us took the risk of hurtling to infinity to try to find Brodix? It would mean one could remain if there happened to be no way of getting back,"

The Amazon said nothing for a moment, then her violet eyes met Abna's levelly.

"We might never meet again," she said at length. "On account of a daughter whom we might never recover, we, too, would voluntarily sever all connection with each other, just when we had planned to do so much. Does that seem right to you?"

"Right or wrong, we cannot leave Viona stranded in some inexplicable mathematical world—or rather void. She is ours, Vi, even if we have to sacrifice everything to bring her back."

The Amazon hesitated, then she frowned as she looked beyond Abna. At her curious expression he glanced ever his shoulder, and remained fixed, watching a haze that was slowly taking form. Upon the floor there began to merge a queer, quivering mass like a pattern of symbols.

"It's Brodix!" the Amazon cried. "That's his mosaic patterner coming into view!"

She hurried to Abna's side and held on to his arm tensely, watching as the weird illusion began to take shape. Like something emerging from mist a figure came into view, his head in a cage, his legs like sawn-off blocks.

"Tarnec Brodix!" Abna strode forward and gripped the scientist's small hand. "Thank the cosmos you got our message."

"Two messages were received," the odd little being responded, his thought waves sharp and incisive. "One by mental force and the other by recorded sound. I was meditating over the first when the second interrupted me. Much time was lost in making up for the gap in mathematical sequence."

"I'm sorry." Abna looked suitably humbled, a giant in front of a sparrow. "I don't need to explain the situation: you know how things are. Somehow Viona mnst be restored."

"To cancel out integrals which have been so carefully established will not be easy," Brodix responded. "I must meditate."

He moved away, head bent forward as far as the cage would allow. Neither the Amazon nor Abna interrupted him. They had come to understand by now just how queerly this alien, super-intelligent being worked.

"I assume that Viona has connection with Quorne?" he asked, without turning.

"Wife," Abna answered bitterly. "Mate, if you prefer."

"And offspring expected," the Amazon added. "We did not know of that when we said Quorne had no entanglements."

"Difficult, difficult," Brodix muttered; then he seemed to make up his mind, for he stood suddenly rigid, head thrust a little forward, his almost hidden eyes peering into distance.

# CHAPTER ELEVEN
## A FEAT PERFORMED

It was not long before the tremendous power of his mental waves brought a hazing of the air in the centre of the room. The haze changed and merged gradually into a moving figure. It crept slowly out of blurred outline into a young woman.

It was Viona, crudely dressed; apparently walking along deliberately yet getting nowhere. Behind her was a desolate plain. Her troubled features were lighted with an unseen sun.

"Viona!" Abna gasped at last, and dived forward.

He never reached her, however. A solid but invisible wall barred his path and brought him crashing to his knees. Dazed, he shook his head and scrambled up.

"Between you and Viona is the barrier of space and time," the mastermind explained. "I have recreated her image so I may see where she is. You cannot touch her or hear her, and she is certainly unaware of us. According to my calculations she has reintegrated in the twenty-fifth plane."

"Then she isn't just a mass of wandering mathematics?" the Amazon asked.

"By no means. Nor is Quorne. Even figures have to reintegrate into a whole—or near whole—otherwise they are inexpressed. Inexpressed mathematics cannot exist. The sum total in the case of Viona has added up in the twenty-fifth plane. Two planes removed from her—the twenty-seventh—Quorne will have reintegrated, except for one factor that I possess. That one factor will prevent him being complete and fill him with that insatiable longing of which I spoke."

"Are Viona and Quorne likely to meet?" Abna asked.

"No. Their fields of action are as apart as the opposite ends of the universe. Viona is still alive, exploring the plane into which she has been flung."

There followed a long silence and the vision of Viona faded into nothing. The room was normal again. The mastermind brooded through a long interval, then at last his thoughts came again.

"Viona can be restored to you, but to her restoration there are conditions," Brodix added.

"Name them!" Abna said promptly. "Whatever recompense you desire, you can have. Everything we possess is yours for the asking in return for your help."

"Nothing you can give me, my friends, can have any value. The conditions are not concerned with me, but with Viona. You must make a choice. If I am to restore Viona to you, I must also restore Quorne."

The Amazon looked at Abna sharply.

"Why is that necessary?" Abna asked.

"Because they are both involved in the same mathematical matrix. If one returns, so must the other."

"Which would put us right back where we started," Abna muttered, and turned away to think the matter out. The Amazon drifted to his side. Behind them, Tarnec Brodix waited impassively, his mind preoccupied with profound problems.

"We have never had an issue like this to settle before, Vi," Abna said. "Of course, we could have Viona back and then deal with Quorne."

"And have him perpetuated through Viona's child?" the Amazon asked.

Abna declared: "We can't let Viona drift away in the unknown just because we don't want Quorne back. They'll both have to return."

The Amazon answered: "You miss one vital fact all the time, Abna. You hate Quorne, and so do I—but Viona's hatred of him is by no means as intense as yours and mine. Suppose she returned and Quorne, too, and we killed him. What would be her reactions? We hope that she would be glad, but she might not. Whatever else he may be, he has made himself her husband. It is obvious that to Viona's inexperienced mind Quorne does not seem so deadly. She thinks of him as a brilliant scientist with a power complex. That, to a girl of Viona's age, is not a very terrible thing. We would seem much more terrible if we killed Quorne."

Abna's look was wondering. "Vi, what does this mean? Are you actually suggesting that we should abandon Viona?"

The Amazon's eyes were resigned, yet adamant. "Yes, I am suggesting it. It is the only way in which peace can ever be preserved in the system. Even if it means losing Viona, we must be rid of Quorne and his possible successor."

"It won't do for me," Abna said. "Viona means more than the system to me, and I want her back."

"If you do that, Abna, you will make us enemies again. I am dedicated to fighting Quorne and all he stands for. I would sacrifice Viona for that, if need be."

"I believe sometimes, Vi, that people are right in what they say of you." Abna said. "You have no humanity, no sense of affection. You will sacrifice anything to a scientific ideal. Well, I won't!"

He swung aside and moved over to where Brodix was standing waiting.

"Would it be possible to make a configuration that would take me into the plane where Viona is?" he asked.

"Yes." Brodix assented. "But is that what you really desire? To me it seems strange that—"

"That is what I want! To bring Viona back here with Quorne would cause trouble, but I don't intend to leave her to fight things by herself. I'm still her father and I mean to join her."

"Abna, you fool!" the Amazon cried, going toward him. "Why do you have to be so impulsive? Think over what I've said and you'll see I'm right."

"All I can see is that you have a heart like an adding machine," he retorted. "If you don't like the idea of my leaving to aid the child who belongs to us, then come with me and help."

The Amazon shook her blonde head. "No, Abna. One of us must stay behind. The people of the system need that. Go on your mission and protect Viona if you can—but don't return with her and bring Quorne also. If that happens, I will destroy Quorne the moment he appears."

"Obviously it was a mistake to give you a daughter," Abna said angrily; then he motioned to Brodix. "The sooner you can transplant me to Viona, Brodix, the better."

"Simply done, my friend," Brodix replied. "But the way back will be complicated, and only I can find it."

"I may not need a way back. I think I have perhaps made a mistake in the woman I chose for a mate."

The emotions of humans, or superhumans, were beyond the interest of Brodix. He concentrated, and by degrees Abna became transparent and at last vanished. The Amazon bit her lower lip and stood in silence as Brodix came toward her.

"I have no wish to question your decision," he said, "but I would remark that according to mathematics you and the man who has just vanished into the twenty-fifth plane were admirably balanced. It is not wise for you to allow your ambitions to diverge."

"He has made his choice, Brodix: I have made mine." The Amazon's voice was taut, her mouth set. "Time will show which of us was right."

Brodix reflected, then asked: "You do not require anything more of me?"

"No, thanks. I know how to reach you if I ever need

you again."

Brodix turned away and stood on his mathematical mosaic. Then in a whirl of configurations he was gone. The Amazon gazed at the empty space and then sighed.

Suddenly everything was vastly lonely. In the course of a few brief weeks she had regained Abna and been given a daughter—and lost both. But she had won the battle against Sefner Quorne.

Or had she? Quorne still lived, and through his progeny, though separated at the moment by dimensions and hyperspace, would by all normal laws come into being one day.... And then?

The Amazon relaxed, lost in speculation.

# ABOUT THE AUTHOR

British writer JOHN RUSSELL FEARN was born near Manchester, England, in 1908. As a child he devoured the science fiction of Wells and Verne, and was a voracious reader of the Boys' Story Papers. He was also fascinated by the cinema, and first broke into print in 1931 with a series of articles in *Film Weekly*.

He then quickly sold his first novel, *The Intelligence Gigantic*, to the American magazine, *Amazing Stories*. Over the next fifteen years, writing under several pseudonyms, Fearn became one of the most prolific contributors to all of the leading US science fiction pulps, including such legendary publications as *Astounding Stories*, *Startling Stories*, *Thrilling Wonder Stories*, and *Weird Tales*.

During the late 1940s he diversified into writing novels for the UK market, and also created his famous superwoman character, The Golden Amazon, for the prestigious Canadian magazine, the Toronto *Star Weekly*. In the early 1950s in the UK, his fifty-two novels as "Vargo Statten" were bestsellers, most notably his novelization of the film, *Creature from the Black Lagoon*.

Apart from science fiction, he had equal success with westerns, romances, and detective fiction, writing an amazing total of 180 novels—most of them in a period of just ten years—before his early death in 1960. His work has been translated into nine languages, and continues to be reprinted and read worldwide.

www.ingramcontent.com/pod-product-compliance
Lightning Source LLC
Chambersburg PA
CBHW050732250626
47155CB00005B/1760